With a swoosh, I parted the

curtains. King lay there with a thick satin blanket covering his torso, his arms to his sides. He looked as beautiful as ever, his lips relaxed, that regal set of straight black brows arched perfectly across his forehead. Thick silky lashes fanned out over his cheekbones, and a wash of inky stubble covered his square jaw. He looked like a sleeping Greek god, too beautiful for words. He was back. Alive again. Shiny new body.

I sighed with relief. "King? Can you hear me?" I sat on the edge of the bed and touched his arm. "King? You're safe now. Sage is gone."

"Mmmm…" he groaned.

"Open your eyes. Tell me you're okay."

Suddenly, his arm reached out and pulled me down. He rolled on top of me, pinning my hands above my head.

"What are you doing?" I gasped.

The blankets were tangled between our bodies, but I could feel he was hard.

King buried his head in the crook of my neck and began kissing the tender skin. "You feel so good. I missed you."

I winced, knowing those words weren't for me. How could they be? His mind was probably off somewhere with Mia.

OTHER WORKS BY MIMI JEAN PAMFILOFF

COMING SOON!

Baby, Please (OHellNo #7) ← Hot guy gets surprise baby.

Wall Men (Wall Men, #1) ← Horror romance. Because why not?

Never King's (King Series #8) ← The last one. I mean it this time? LOL

Just Mr. Love (RevoLUVtion #2) ← Huff is taking off the gloves!

The Immortal Tailor (Immortal Tailor, #1) ← Hot immortal men, anyone?

She's Got the Time (M.O. Mack, Suite #45 Series) ← Sounds like Emily's in trouble again.

THE ACCIDENTALLY YOURS SERIES

(Paranormal Romance/Humor)

Accidentally in Love with…a God? (Book 1)

Accidentally Married to…a Vampire? (Book 2)

Sun God Seeks…Surrogate? (Book 3)

Accidentally…Evil? (Novella, Book 3.5)

Vampires Need Not…Apply? (Book 4)

Accidentally…Cimil? (Novella, Book 4.5)

Accidentally…Over? (Finale, Book 5)

THE BOYFRIEND COLLECTOR DUET

(New Adult/Suspense)

The Boyfriend Collector, Part 1

The Boyfriend Collector, Part 2

FANGED LOVE
(Standalone/Paranormal/Humor)

THE FATE BOOK DUET
(New Adult/Humor)
Fate Book
Fate Book Two

THE FUGLY DUET
(Contemporary Romance)
fugly
it's a fugly life

THE HAPPY PANTS SERIES
(Standalones/Romantic Comedy)
The Happy Pants Café (Prequel)
Tailored for Trouble (Book 1)
Leather Pants (Book 2)
Skinny Pants (Book 3)

IMMORTAL MATCHMAKERS, INC., SERIES
(Standalones/Paranormal/Humor)
The Immortal Matchmakers (Book 1)
Tommaso (Book 2)
God of Wine (Book 3)
The Goddess of Forgetfulness (Book 4)
Colel (Book 5)
Brutus (Book 6)
God of Temptation (Finale)

THE KING SERIES
(Dark Fantasy/Suspense)
King's (Book 1)
King for a Day (Book 2)
King of Me (Book 3)
Mack (Book 4)
Ten Club (Book 5)
The Dead King (Book 6)
Lord King (Book 7) ← You are here!
Never King's (Book 8) ← Coming 2022.

THE LIBRARIAN'S VAMPIRE ASSISTANT
(Standalones/Mystery/Humor)
The Librarian's Vampire Assistant (Book 1)
The Librarian's Vampire Assistant (Book 2)
The Librarian's Vampire Assistant (Book 3)
The Librarian's Vampire Assistant (Book 4)
The Librarian's Vampire Assistant (Book 5)
Vampire Man (Book 6, FINALE)

THE MERMEN TRILOGY
(Dark Fantasy/Suspense)
Mermen (Part 1)
MerMadmen (Part 2)
MerCiless (Part 3)

MR. ROOK'S ISLAND TRILOGY
(Contemporary/Suspense)
Mr. Rook (Part 1)
Pawn (Part 2)
Check (Part 3)

THE OHELLNO SERIES
(Standalones/New Adult/Romantic Comedy)
Smart Tass (Book 1)
Oh Henry (Book 2)
Digging A Hole (Book 3)
Battle of the Bulge (Book 4)
My Pen is Huge (Book 5)
Wine Hard, Baby (Book 6)
Baby, Please (Book 7) ← COMING SOON!

REVOLUVTION SERIES
(Romance/Action/Dark Humor)
Mr. Ultra Mega Love (Book 1)
Just Mr. Love (Book 2) ← Coming 2022.

SUITE #45 SERIES by M.O. MACK
(Thriller/Suspense/Action)
She's Got the Guns (Book 1)
She's Got the Money (Book 2)
She's Got the Time (Book 3) ← Coming 2022.

WISH, a Standalone Novel
(Romantic Comedy)

LORD KING

Mimi Jean Pamfiloff

A Mimi Boutique Novel

Cover Design: Earthly Charms & Sweet 'N Spicy Designs
Developmental Editing: Stephanie Elliot
Copyediting and Proof Reading: Pauline Nolet & JRT Editing
Formatting: Paul Salvette

LORD KING

CHAPTER ONE

As sloppy raindrops pelted my windshield, I watched my newest discovery emerge from her hotel and hurry down the wet sidewalk. She wore spiked heels and a skimpy black cocktail dress, far too sexy for eight o'clock in the morning and entirely the wrong outfit for this weather.

"What are you up to, my little treasure?" My grip tightened around the steering wheel. I suspected she was going to meet *him*, the man I would kill within a matter of days.

And sorry, King, but winner takes all. Soon, she would be mine, and I had big plans for my little treasure.

Fact was, her breed of power deserved to be wielded by someone with ambition, someone who was born to lead, a ruthless bastard through and through. Me.

He'll never want you anyway, my little treasure. Not even her sexy black dress, displaying the sensual roundness of her large breasts, could entice a man such as King. The soulless. The cursed. The man who claimed he could find anything or anyone. For a price. But he would never find an appreciation for her as I would.

A Seer. A real-life fucking Seer. Just what I needed to complete my arsenal of weapons. Because like King, I was a treasure hunter. I'd dedicated almost two thousand years of my existence to seeking a way to end my tortured, hollow existence. Until one day, I found it, and for the first time since my mother cursed me, I had control.

That was the moment I began living. Truly living. Because I finally understood power was everything. Being on top was everything.

Now the pieces were falling into place. King had recently ended Ten Club. He'd murdered all but three of its members, me being one of them, and I couldn't be happier.

Such a gift you've given me, King. He was clearing the way so I could build my own dream.

All I needed now was for King to finish off the other two members—a pair of depraved assholes who would give him a run for his money.

Pure entertainment. Fights like those, between individuals with supernatural arsenals that could destroy a small country, only came along once in a lifetime.

After that, King would come for me, but I wouldn't lose.

I swiped my hand across the fogging windshield to watch the keystone of my future disappear down the steep San Francisco street. *Jeni, you and I are going to change the world.*

JENI

Dripping wet, I ducked inside the postage-stamp-sized lobby of the old brick building that had been converted to loft spaces and then left vacant for decades by its owner: King. Now back from the dead. Again.

I wrung my long hair, attempting to dispel some of the rain. Wet weather wasn't typical for San Francisco at this time of year, but what did I know? I was from Tallahassee, Florida, where we received most of our rain during hurricane season, which was how I met King.

Hurricane Mia had delivered him to the port where I was working on a cleanup crew after Tampa had been obliterated. We were some of the first people in, clearing debris and downed cranes so emergency supplies could get in by boat. When King washed ashore inside a steel box, everyone assumed he was dead, but they couldn't have been more wrong.

King was incapable of dying.

I peeled the front of my wet dress from my chest. "What a mess." I knew my makeup was a lost cause, as were my new black heels. King was well over six feet, and I barely reached his pecs. I thought the shoes might make him take another look at me.

I'm ridiculous. He could never want me. His heart belonged to his dead wife, Mia, and the only thing he cared about, besides her and his dead children, was to die and join them on the other side.

Okay. Fine. I supposed Ariadna, his daughter, wasn't really dead. Like me, she was a Seer, and according to them, we could never truly die. Our souls migrated to Seer-land or wherever the fuck we went—some plane between this world and the next that sounded suspiciously like purgatory.

The only exception I knew of was King's late wife, Mia, who gave up her Seer powers. Why? Not sure, but I did know she was beyond this realm and beyond his reach.

I made another swipe over my dress, using my hands as squeegees, but it was no use. I was soaked to the bone.

I walked over to the shiny elevator doors and pushed the up button on the wall. The wet racoon with stringy dark hair, staring back in the reflection, confirmed my ridiculous decision to not check the weather before I left this morning, along with my pathetic choice to dress like I was going to a nightclub at eight in the morning.

I could return to my hotel room for a change of clothes, but I was already late, and King waited for no man.

I reached into my oversized leather purse and dug out my pack of travel tissues to blot my face.

The elevator doors chimed and slid open.

"Good morning, Jeni." A pair of haunting pale gray eyes stared from inside the elevator.

"King!" I jumped in my sloshy heels, my heart going crazy. Half due to shock, half because King was a mysterious man who exuded a deadly vibe, all wrapped up in the timeless masculine beauty of an old-world god.

Of course, if you passed him on the street, all you'd see was a wealthy modern businessman dressed in a fine Italian suit. You'd notice his stunningly handsome face, too—the elegant cheekbones, the lips and regal nose. But if you looked closely, deep into his eyes, you'd sense he wasn't entirely of this world. And you'd be right.

In truth, he was once Draco Minos, an ancient Minoan king with powers I would never begin to understand. He was also my lifeline in this dangerous world I'd recently discovered I belonged to.

"Run into a waterfall on your way here?" He cocked a black brow that matched the inky stubble on his exquisite jawline.

Why does he have to be so beautiful?

A sly smile crept across his lips. "You know I can hear your thoughts, Jeni."

And I can hear yours, too. I folded my bare arms across my chest to hide my nipples, which were surely poking out from being wet and cold.

"I am aware." He dipped his head. "Though, I should inform you I have been around for over three thousand years, and you are not the first woman I've met with such a talent."

"And?"

"And…" He stepped from the elevator, pressing his body flush with mine.

Too close for comfort to a man I didn't trust, I stepped back, landing right in the puddle I'd just left from my dripping clothes. My heel slid out from under me on the slick tile. "Oh crap!"

"Careful now." In a blink, King had me in his arms, his body bowed over mine as if he were dipping me on a dance floor during tango night.

My eyes locked on his, my heart thumping even louder in response to the darkness inside him. Was he a man, ghost, monster? Something in between? My body didn't seem to fucking care because the slideshow of memories began: our sweat-slicked naked bodies writhing, the exquisite muscles of his chest and arms as he glided over me, thrusting relentlessly, and the sound of his heavy breaths filling my ears as he came.

It had only been a few weeks since he'd fucked me so hard that he'd left an indelible mark on my soul, but things couldn't be more different now.

Now, he remembered who he was, and the stranger I'd first met, who washed ashore in a metal box, was long gone. Now, he was King, the man who defied all laws—natural, moral, or otherwise.

As for me, things were different, too. For starters, discovering I was a Seer—the only one alive, thanks to King, who'd killed them off after a major falling-out. Two, realizing I was in love with an ancient king who would never love me back. Three, learning that if I cared about King, I had to help him find redemption for three thousand years of twisted behavior that had left behind a deep and terrible footprint on the world. And, finally, being told by the "dead" Seers they'd bound his soul to me. I was what anchored him to a world he so badly wanted to vacate. To die, he needed that bond broken. And to do that, he had to make things right with the Seers. The irony was that I didn't want to lose him.

Fucking fate. You're a stone-cold bitch.

"My, my, such foul language, Jeni." King slowly released me from his grip, pulling me upright. "But let us get one thing straight: I am evil. Evil as I am powerful."

I already knew that. I also knew there was a part of him that loved his wife so deeply he'd managed to cheat death just to have more time with her. A man who loved so profoundly couldn't be all bad.

"Your point?" I said.

He leaned closer, speaking with a menacing tone. "Just because I loved my wife or am seeking redemption doesn't change what I am. I would slit your throat, Jeni. I would trade you away to the vilest of men. I would betray you in a heartbeat if it meant getting what I want. Never forget that."

I furrowed my brows, wondering how I could

love such a dark creature.

"A valid question," he said, responding to my thoughts. "You should also ask yourself why you put on such a seductive dress this morning. Perhaps you think a part of me wanted you once, and it will do so again. But the man I was when we met wasn't real, and you know that."

Ashamed, I looked away. I didn't like how King could hear my thoughts. But I *hated* how he used them against me.

He grabbed my chin, forcing me to meet his icy pale gray gaze. "I'm not worth your heart, Jeni."

"Only, you don't dictate what I feel." Neither did I. When it came to him, my heart had a will of its own.

His gaze softened. "Then you understand when I say my heart is bound only to Mia. So, if I must die to see her or our son, Arch, again, so be it."

Arch was his infant son, killed twenty-five years ago by the Seers on the same night they took Mia's life. Why did they do that?

According to King, he'd had the bright idea of resurrecting the most ancient and powerful of our kind and then forced them to work as his supernatural thugs so he could keep control over Ten Club.

What was Ten Club? Basically, King's monster.

Try to imagine a group of extremely powerful, corrupt billionaires with sick, dark fetishes and an unchecked lust for power. Some members purely wanted to be above the law, but others became bored over time and turned to the occult.

Ten Club was a sort of group insurance plan. They each paid an annual fee of ten billion dollars into a pool managed by King, and with that, he bought them complete immunity. He offered favors, bought off judges and politicians, or had people disappear. Whatever it took to protect the members, who in turn could kidnap, kill, entrance, enslave, rape, torture, or do anything their hearts desired. *Sick.*

Of course, the Seers didn't appreciate being brought back from the dead or being enslaved by King to help him keep Ten Club in check. It all ended badly. They rose up. He killed the Seers, but a few got away first and took out their revenge on his family. Their infant son and King's pregnant wife.

Sad. So sad. A Greek tragedy if I'd ever heard one.

What got me was how Seers were female healers who supposedly brought balance to the world. So why kill King's family and not him? Especially because Mia had been pregnant with Ariadna, a Seer. Pretty damn messed up, if you asked me.

Now Ariadna's soul or light or whatever they called it was a young woman, living with my sisters in Seer-land. I wondered what growing up there instead of here had been like. The two worlds were completely different.

"You are correct," King said, listening to me

rattle on inside my head. "Ariadna was robbed of her human experience due to my poor choices, which is why I do not deserve her devotion. She's hope where there is none to be had."

None? What about me, King? I'm here to help you die when it kills me to think of a world without you in it.

King stared but said nothing.

I inhaled slowly. "All I'm asking is that you stop dismissing me. I can't help how I feel any more than you can help wanting to see Mia again." I shook my head, my wet sloppy hair sliding across my shoulders. "I'm here to help you redeem yourself and find your way back to your family." That was what the Seers had asked me to do, and I was going to do it.

He opened his mouth to speak just as a menacing shadow darted across the lobby and began circling him.

Oh god! I stepped back toward the door, my neck and arms exploding with goosebumps. I'd seen the shadow before, right after I met King. At first I thought it'd been my imagination, but then I found out it was his tortured soul detached from his body. It was every piece of King that didn't belong to the world of the living, yet his flesh and bone could draw on those powers. That was how he'd taken out Ten Club. He'd summoned them and let his shadow loose. They never saw it coming.

The shadow zipped past my head, leaving an ice-cold trail across my damp cheek.

"My soul is eager to return to its owner," King said calmly, his eyes following the thing around the room. "It is anxious to put an end to the Seers' punishment."

This is so fucking weird. "Then let's get started. What's first?" I couldn't get rid of that thing fast enough. Not that it followed me around all hours of the day, but late at night, when the air was still and everything was quiet, sometimes I felt it lurking. Creepy as hell.

"First, we hunt down the three remaining Ten Club members," said King. "Then we go from there to try to correct some of my misdeeds."

"I'm sorry, but what? You never mentioned anyone survived."

"Three members did not answer my summons for the meeting that night and still roam free."

Guess not all Ten Club members are complete idiots. Why hadn't he said something?

"Because one of them is Victor Escorcia."

"What?" My heart lit up with red-hot rage. I wasn't a violent person, but if I were a god who could smite anyone on this earth with a flick of a pinky, I'd flick away at Victor Escorcia. The animal murdered my mother. "Do you know where to find him?"

"I do. But let's get one thing straight, Jeni; no matter how much you hate the man, you are to leave the killing to me."

Have you ever had a fist shoved up your ass?

King shrugged his dark silky brows. "Pardon me?"

"Just answer the question," I growled.

"No," he replied sternly.

"Would you like to?" I clenched my fist and shook it at him. "Because I just discovered my secret Seer power."

King reached out and clasped my wrist. "Are you threatening me with a fist fuck? Are you insane, woman?"

"Try me."

With a frustrated groan, King dropped my arm. "I do not have time for this, Seer."

"Victor Escorcia took everything from my father. He took everything from me. I *will* kill him, and you have no right to stand in my way." Especially because King had promised he'd take care of Victor. Now, the man was running around free again? The most evil, vile person ever to walk the earth?

"And," King added, "he was your catalyst, your spark toward greatness."

"Are *you* fucking insane?"

"You studied history, so you will comprehend when I say that every hero, every great man or woman—from the fictional god to the legendary historical figures who triumphed against all odds—had their moment of transformation. They faced the worst this world has to offer and rose like a phoenix." He pressed his index finger over my heart. "To soar high, you must know hell. That knowledge will drive you to remain above it."

I frowned. "You're saying I need to suffer to know how much I want to avoid it?"

King nodded.

That's the stupidest thing I've ever heard. "I don't need to be skinned alive to understand how shitty that would feel. Same goes for having my hands chopped off or being forced to listen to you preach to me. I'm perfectly capable of imagining all the fucked-up things I can live without."

"You think you're funny, Seer?" King reached forward, wrapping his large hand around my neck. "This isn't a game, Jeni. My eternity is on the line, and I will do this my way."

I pushed his hands away. "That's my point. You're the one with everything on the line. Three thousand years of crap to repent for. So why pile on? Let *me* kill Victor."

With a low growl he said, "Not that I am obligated to explain myself, but if you kill Victor Escorcia, it would merely be an act of revenge. Ending Ten Club is *my* penance."

"Don't care. I want to kill him."

"You say that; however, until you have killed hundreds of times, it will haunt you. Ending Victor will be nothing for me. I've killed for power. I've killed to protect what's mine. I've even killed for amusement. To me, death is a tool to get what I want. It's like an old friend."

I tried not to laugh. "A little ironic since death is the only thing in this world you can't have for yourself."

"I always get what I want. Eventually." He smiled with a bitter twitch.

I froze, fixated on those full, sensual lips. I couldn't ignore the underlying pull I constantly felt lurking beneath the surface. Memories of his mouth on mine flashed in my head.

"I am not a man to love, Jeni. What must I do to convince you? Should I slit your throat? Kill your father? Perhaps I should maim that lovely face of yours."

"You think you scare me?"

He wrapped his hand around my throat again, slamming me back against the wall just opposite the elevators. Hard veins popped from his temples. "I could crush your neck, Jeni. Right here. Right now."

King had tried to scare me into obedience before. Sadly for him, I knew this trick. "You're nothing but a little dog, King. All bark. Tiny bite."

He gripped my neck tighter, pulled me forward, and slammed me again to the wall. "Stop provoking me, Seer."

It was my turn to flash a taunting smile. The problem was, I could hear his thoughts now. I could see inside his heart, just like he could see inside mine. I'd recently discovered that this was my gift: seeing through the walls around people's hearts. It was why I'd shielded myself from the world up until the moment King washed ashore. I feared what was in people's minds, so I blocked them out, kept my distance.

"I'm sorry, King," I reached out, covering his heart with my hand, "but like it or not, you can't hide from me. I see you. You see me. We. Are. Connected."

"Bullshit!" *The only woman I am connected to is Mia.*

"Wrong," I replied to his thoughts. "She is the only woman you love. But I know you feel something for me, just like I do for you. All I'm asking is—"

"What? A fucking fairy tale? I am a king, not a prince."

"I know you won't ever love me like you do her or your children. I happen to admire you for being so loyal. But I also know I don't deserve your hate." I tilted my head to the side, keeping my palm flat over his beating heart, a heart that should've stopped over three thousand years ago, but kept on pumping for love. How could King not see how miraculous that was?

He stepped back. "If you *see* so much, then tell me why you are still holding out hope that I will stay here with you, in the land of the living, instead of crossing over to be with my wife?"

I knew why I couldn't stop hoping, and I'd spent the last week learning how to shield the answer from him. I'd imagined a fortress made of steel bricks, five layers deep, and placed my most important thoughts and secrets inside. Apparently, the trick worked because King had no idea I was pregnant. With his baby. I already felt the intense power growing inside, which meant it had to be a girl, a Seer just like me.

And he can't find out.

I refused to be his pity side piece, holding him to a world he didn't want to be in, with a woman he could never love.

"I'm just here to help, King. Nothing more."

CHAPTER TWO
KING

Help? I do not need her help. I had already sent Jeni home to Florida once, and now she was back, hiding something. I could feel it. Yet I sensed nothing malicious in her actions, which meant her secret had to do with one of two things: her heart or her fear of losing me.

I knew she had fallen in love with me the night we fucked, but that changed nothing. I could never love her back. Mia was and would always be my soul, my heart, my purpose for existing. The best I could offer Jeni was my honesty, and I had.

As for her fear of my leaving this world, she would get over it. Everything still felt new to her, but with time, she would come into her own as a Seer. I was not here to assist with that. My goal was dying. Preferably sooner rather than later. The challenge was, I kept coming back to life—a punishment inflicted upon me by the ancient Seers—and it would continue happening until those fucking witches untethered my soul from Jeni or I found a way to break their curse. In either case, Jeni's help would only be a liability. Also, I did not trust her. Seers were devious. Even the good ones.

"Where are you staying?" I asked Jeni.

"At a hotel down the street. Why?"

"Give me the address. Then go there and get packed. I will be along shortly to retrieve you."

"Where are we going?"

"*You* are going home." I was not about to take her along to hunt down the three remaining Ten Club members. These individuals had not avoided death out of luck. They were crafty and underhanded, and they would be expecting me. Obviously, I could not die, but Jeni could. Yes, hers would be a Seer's death, but her time in this world would cease prematurely—something I did not want.

In my experience, Seers who'd lived long lives in this world were Seers who accepted their place in the endless Seer afterlife. Those who died too young were restless, obsessing over all the experiences they missed out on—love, having families, and growing old. I did not wish a tormented afterlife for Jeni.

"You will go home, Seer," I said, "and I will carry out my penance. *Alone.*"

Jeni shrugged her light brown eyebrows. "I thought I made myself clear, King. I'm coming along."

"You will only get in the way."

"If you're hunting down the man who murdered my mother, there's nothing you can say or do to stop me from going with you."

I tilted my head at the stubborn woman. *You know very well I can do many things.*

"Why are you being such an asshole? Victor Escorcia ran my mother over just for fun. He deserves a painful, terrifying death."

"Indeed. And I will ensure he receives it without you interfering, which I am certain you will do." Jeni was becoming quite the ballsy woman now, very different from the helpless mouse I first met, who could hardly speak above a whisper or look a person in the eyes. Now she was turning into a fighter.

"Give me one good reason why, King? Why can't I at least come with you and watch Victor take his last breath?"

I stared into Jeni's golden-brown eyes. So full of life, this one. *And thirsty for vengeance, too.* I found it very attractive, but not enough to act on it again. "Victor is not your usual Ten Club member. None of the three remaining individuals are."

"How?"

"Victor was married to Serina, and she had a most impressive arsenal."

Serina had taken over Ten Club during my long absence—a "vacation" at the bottom of the ocean. It had been my attempt to end my suffering after my family was killed. Did not work, of course, and ironically, Hurricane Mia had washed me to shore and served me up to Jeni.

"You killed Serina the night of the Ten Club massacre," Jeni said. "So what's your point?"

"My point is that Victor is now in possession of every artifact, every item of power Serina amassed."

"You think he might hurt me," Jeni concluded.

I nodded. "Me as well." I doubted he could kill me, for obvious reasons, but that didn't mean he couldn't subdue or torture me for a few millennia. The cold truth was, I had done the same to others. I feared such a fate. No end. Just pain.

"I'm coming anyway." Jeni narrowed her eyes. "The ancient ones ordered me to stay by your side and ensure there's no funny business. No detours. No double-crossing."

"You do not trust me?" Good for her.

"What I think doesn't matter."

I inhaled deeply through my nostrils. The Seers knew I could tell them to go fuck themselves. With the power I had, I could ward the entire planet and block them from ever returning.

Of course, they were not without their own bag of tricks. It was their curse keeping me here.

"I doubt the ancient ones wish you to join me for a killing," I pointed out.

"Then I agree to leave the murdering to you, but I'm coming along. Fair 'nuff?"

I nodded, not wishing to waste more time. My soul and mind were restless. My heart grew weaker by the day from the darkness inside, eating away at it. Without Mia to keep me grounded, I feared my time to find redemption—or even care about it—was growing short.

"Well?" Jeni prodded. "Do we have a deal? Because I want the last thing he sees to be my face smiling down and telling him how worthless his pathetic fuck of a life was."

Hell, she is getting dark. I liked it. "Fair enough."

"Great. So where's Victor?"

"Miami." He had to know I was coming for him. All three surviving members of Ten Club had to know. They hadn't risen to their places in Ten Club—the most untrustworthy, depraved, power-hungry psychopaths ever to walk the earth—by being foolish. Which was why I wasn't going to Miami to simply kill Victor. I was going for a fight, my triumph not guaranteed.

CHAPTER THREE
JENI

Victor Escorcia. Where to start? I guessed a good place was explaining how he got drunk one night and ran over my mother with his car. My father had to raise me alone and never quite got over losing her. So, basically, my childhood sucked. But the devastating impact Victor had on the world didn't end there.

Just a few short weeks ago, I discovered he'd killed tons of women. It was his favorite pastime, and Ten Club protected him. That was why Victor never went to prison for murdering Mom.

I just wished I understood why King had created that organization to begin with. What the fuck was he thinking? I guessed it didn't matter now because he ultimately lost everything over his choices, and what was done was done. Now he had to clean up his evil mess.

How?

I only knew a small part of the Seers' plan. King had to destroy any evidence of his evil existence. In addition, the Seers wanted to come back. Yes, to this world. Alive. They claimed the world needed them to help repair the harm King'd done—"set our fates on a different path" they'd said. Seemed like a damned big undertaking to me, but what did I know?

King and I slipped into his black Mercedes sedan parked along the alley behind his office building. A light drizzle fell from the sky, and I was still soaked, which was probably why King put his coat on the passenger seat.

"So, no more chauffeurs?" I asked as he took the wheel. The last time we were together, he'd had servants at his beck and call. The weird part was they'd all had the last name of Spiros. All of them Greek.

"The days of servants, subjects, and kingdoms are over for me," he said.

Maybe so, but he was still a king. The Seers were counting on his leadership when they returned—something I didn't understand.

"What was that?" he asked.

"The Seers are counting on you to make things right," I said. "So we should get moving. Lots to do."

He turned his head and stared deep into my eyes. "What aren't you telling me, Seer?"

"My name is Jeni." *Same name you groaned into my ear when you were comi—*

"Enough," he snarled.

I smiled coolly. I enjoyed getting under his skin, especially now that we were on an even playing field when it came to what went on inside each other's heads. One could even argue I had a leg up. I could hide things.

"Which is why I will ask you once again, *Jeni*; what are you keeping from me?"

My mind quickly shuffled. The real secret was in my belly, but I could never tell him. "It's no secret. You're just not ready to hear it yet," I lied, hoping he'd think my thoughts had something to do with the Seers' plans for him.

King narrowed those hypnotic pale eyes. "I do not like your kind, Jeni. And I like your games even less."

"Why, King? Why do you hate Seers? Is it because you couldn't tame us? Is it because the ancient ones refused to be your obedient slaves?"

"Seers killed my family."

That part I completely got. "But this started a long time ago, right? What happened? How did they all die to begin with? Why did you bring a bunch of them back from the dead?" He must've known it wouldn't end well.

"It is a long story; however, not all of the women were disappointed about returning. It was only a handful."

"So some were actually glad to be raised from the dead to work for you?"

"One in particular insisted upon it. She believed

her place was at my side."

So I wasn't the first Seer to have a thing for the enigma known as King. "But then why kill them all after their attempted takeover of Ten Club? Why not just remove the ones who moved against you?"

"I no longer required their services, and frankly, I was not in the mood to ascertain if any were worth keeping. I simply wished to dismantle Ten Club— something I promised my wife I would do long ago."

The Seers had told me about this. They said he'd lied to Mia and told her Ten Club no longer existed, but he'd been running it behind her back. She found out and left him. King tried to make things right so he could get her back, but that was when everything went to shit. The Seers found out King was about to pull the plug and send them back to Seer-land, but then they decided they wanted to rule the most violent group of individuals on the planet.

That was another piece I didn't understand. I'd been given the impression my kind wasn't violent.

"Were you not just begging me to let you kill Victor Escorcia five minutes ago?" King asked, listening in on my head chatter.

"Good point."

"Seers are human beings, Jeni. No different than anyone else except for their abilities. They must choose which path they take in life."

So, basically, if I wanted to turn into a raging

psycho-bitch and kill anyone I pleased, I could?

"I never said there weren't consequences for your choices," King added. "Seers have laws, and they punish those who break them."

Why hadn't anyone told me this? "What laws?"

"Best you ask them. I would not wish to incorrectly inform you. Also, I was never one for rules. I have always been more of the breaking type."

Yes, I know. King did what he wanted when he wanted. That defiant strength was what attracted me to him even when I loathed him for his sometimes reckless ways.

"I am *not* the reckless man you think me, Jeni." He exhaled slowly. "Now, I have entertained your questions, and we have work to do. Are you going to answer my question?" *What are you hiding?* He stared expectantly.

This again. I had to tell him something. Anything but the truth. "Uh, well, I'm not really sure it's a secret; I just don't have all the information. The Seers are planning their return."

He cocked a dark silky brow. "Are they now? And how will they manage this?"

I shrugged. I wasn't exactly sure. I only knew they expected King to lead them, which was insane. Why would they want the person who murdered them to be their "lord," as they called him?

"Because I am still their king," he said. "And they want things made right—the king and his Seers shaping the world."

"But you guys have so much bad blood between you."

"Yes, and had I not veered down the path I ultimately took, things would have resulted differently. For them. For me. For the world."

"So they think you have some sort of unfulfilled obligation," I concluded.

"Something like that," he replied in his usual dismissive tone like he couldn't give two fucks about any of this. He just wanted to get back to Mia and Arch.

"You understand me well," he said.

I laughed. "Sure. Right."

King cranked the engine, and the car purred to life. "Next time you speak with your sisters, kindly inform them there's not a chance in hell I'll be their lord. I don't give a fuck if they find a way to come back and reestablish themselves in the world. They can find another leader."

My skin began to tingle. And not in a good way. It was as if some part of me, which was connected to my "sisters," was not happy with what King just said.

"So are you ready to kill some very bad people, little Seer?"

I narrowed my eyes at the beautiful man behind the wheel pulling into traffic. "I need to stop by my hotel and grab my stuff." I was still damp and cold. And this was not the outfit I wanted to wear when I watched Victor Escorcia take his last breath.

A valid point. "He does not deserve such a lovely vision comforting him as I choke the life from his body," King muttered.

I stared for a moment, wondering if he was being sarcastic. But he wasn't. Serious as a heart attack.

And speaking of hearts, mine did a little flutter.

Pathetic. One nice word from King, and I was going all warm and gooey inside. I needed to let go of my feelings for him. If only I knew why I was so attached, I might find a way to break his spell over me.

CHAPTER FOUR

Jeans and a plain red T-shirt. That was what Victor would see on my body as King took his life. He'd also witness my big fat smile.

Maybe I was being vindictive, but what Victor stole couldn't be paid back with his death. Victor's actions had left a gaping, festering hole in my and my dad's lives. He robbed the world of my mom, a person who spent every Sunday reading to people in hospice care. She gave blood once a month and saved up every winter to buy coats just for donation. She was good people.

Meanwhile, Victor lived like royalty on his yacht in Miami. I knew because I'd stalked him online a few times and contemplated paying him a visit long before I met King.

Back then, I was never brave enough to go after Victor. Now I'd tear his head off given the chance. Especially after King told me—and my dad confirmed—that Victor actually showed up drunk to our house one day when I was still little and offered my dad money. "Compensation" for our loss. Victor also offered to take me off my dad's hands—best schools, best clothes, a life of luxury.

Bullshit. I knew what sort of monster Victor was. He would *not* have taken care of me. Raped, beaten, killed, yes. Luckily, my dad loved me and told Victor to fuck off. But why did I get the impression that I wasn't the first or the last little girl Victor attempted to acquire for his sick fantasies?

"Yes, you are quite fortunate your father did not fall for Victor's tricks," King said as we settled into his private jet—one of many, I guessed. This particular plane had leather seats that faced each other. Awkward.

"Victor would have made you his pet," King added.

"I don't even want to think about it." *Especially the part about you protecting that nasty fucker.*

"I did what I must to protect my family. So I believed." Seated across from me, King stared over my head toward the cockpit, his mind somewhere else.

Probably with Mia.

A pang of jealousy speared my heart. "Well, awesome you, because *my* family paid the price." Had Victor gone to jail the first time he broke the law, my life would have been very different.

"I am aware." King still refrained from looking at me. "And when you have lived for three thousand years, witnessing the cruelty, violence, and evil of men, then come see me."

"What's that supposed to mean?"

"Sir." The pilot came up behind me. He was some private contractor. "We're cleared for departure."

King gave him a nod and then lowered his eyes, hitting me with his ice-cold gaze. "The world is full of Victors and always has been. Always will be. There is nothing I can do to change that."

"I understand, but—"

"But nothing, Jeni," he spat. "You know *nothing* other than the few decades you've been alive. You were not around before Jesus, electricity, and guns, when people killed with rocks and bare hands simply because they felt like it. You have never witnessed entire tribes wiped out—women raped, children split in half to extract their beating hearts, the men slowly cooked alive—because another group wanted to appease their gods. I have lived through the Bronze Age, the Dark Ages, and the Industrial Revolution. I was there for the Spanish Inquisition, the European discovery of your continent, and the first man on the moon. I have seen empires rise and fall—Egyptians, Maya, Romans, and Vikings. I have seen the worst this world has to offer, and I have seen it again and again and again. *You* are a child. *You* believe laws will protect you, that people will protect you.

"It is a fantasy, Seer, a myth perpetuated by your foolish Hollywood movies. And if you doubt me, take two steps outside your precious reality. The true nature of man is still alive and well. Drug cartels, gangs, human trafficking, tribal genocide, dictatorships. *That* is reality, woman. People do not change. Evil never goes away. Power, corruption, and greed are the sickness of every generation, of every culture, of every tribe.

"The only thing that can protect you is being deadlier and more powerful than everyone else. And just where the *fuck* do you think you learn to be like that, Seer? At church? Or perhaps in those history books you spent four years of your life studying?" He leaned in. "If you truly wish to survive, you must surround yourself with the worst of the worst, Jeni. The most treacherous, violent, despicable human beings, and you must learn what they do and how they do it. And then you must be better at it than they are. You must outsmart them, obtain better weapons, and sell your fucking soul to the fucking devil for powers that will keep them in their place—fearing you, two steps behind you, or under your foot, gasping for air."

My mouth flapped for several moments. Even if I didn't entirely agree, his words felt like a hard slap of cold truth. I'd been alive for a little over two decades, and up until a few weeks ago, I still believed that when people died, they stayed dead. I believed that while the system wasn't perfect, justice existed. I thought humanity was making strides toward a better place. As a history major in college, I often reveled in the magnitude of mankind's progress.

Now I was learning it was all an illusion. The world was just as dangerous as ever. *Only bigger and messier. Evolution on steroids.*

"A well-placed observation," King said. "Except that the word *evolution* implies change is permanent, like a caterpillar turning into a butterfly. No going back. Mankind has not evolved. It is still made up of two kinds of people: those who wish to be good, and those who will always seek to take power for themselves. The latter never rest. Which is why you must never stop protecting what's yours in this world. Turn your head for one moment, and I guarantee the Victors will be ready. Spears out. Cocks out. Chains ready."

I'd just been given a lesson from a living piece of history, and I wasn't sure if I liked what he'd said.

"The sooner you accept the facts, the better off you'll be," King said bluntly. "In time, you will discover there is very little goodness in the world, and when you find it, you will sacrifice anything to protect it, even if it means becoming the devil to rule the demons. *That* is why I started Ten Club."

The plane's engines revved for takeoff, and I turned my head to stare out the window at the overcast sky. I knew he was right. The baby growing inside me would be one of the good things I would fight tooth and nail for.

I pushed away my thought, not wanting to tip King off.

"Tip me off about what?" he asked.

Fuck. Fuck. I quickly switched gears, diverting my thoughts to something that wasn't a secret. I thought about how much I wanted him and how much I hated the fact he was going to leave me. I never asked to discover what I was. I never asked to meet him. I never wanted any of it.

"You are a peculiar woman, Jeni Arnold."

"Why?"

"I have spent my existence seeking power. I have fought, bartered, killed, and paid dearly for every ounce of it. But you?" He chuckled with disapproval. "Destiny has served it to you on a silver platter, yet you complain."

"I'm not complaining."

"Aren't you?" He narrowed his eyes.

Okay. I guessed I was. Anything to keep my mind away from my secret.

He added, "Perhaps you wish to go back to being the girl I met, who allowed everyone to treat her like a doormat."

Never.

"Then start embracing your powers. You are going to need them," he said.

King claimed I needed to protect myself. Okay. How? So far, my Seer gift made me a human lie detector. *Not exactly lethal.* Also, nothing like King's shadow, which was deadlier than any weapon I'd ever seen. It could rip a person to pieces, pluck out their eyes, and crush their hearts in the blink of an eye. And it had come to my aid several times.

"What happens if you move on before I'm ready?" I asked. "I'll be a Seer without a way to defend myself."

"Life is full of challenges, Seer. Better get used to it." King leaned back and shut his eyes while I fixated on his beautiful face. Part of me still couldn't believe he was as old as he said. He looked to be in his early thirties, nowhere near ready to die.

"I assure you I am ready," he muttered. "Now, if you do not mind, I must gather my strength. Victor will not go down easily."

I was about to ask what King planned to do to Victor but stopped myself. King wasn't going to waste his breath explaining details.

"And you would be right, Jeni." He cracked open a pale gray eye. "Get some rest. Your light is flickering."

"My light?" I questioned.

He ignored me. *Of course.* King wasn't going to waste his breath explaining the Seer world to me either. Not when he hated them so much. They'd killed his wife and babies. They stood between him and the peace his soul yearned for.

CHAPTER FIVE

Just before ten p.m., King and I were in a car, traveling toward the Royal Palms Marina and Yacht Club, where the rich docked their aquatic mansions and enjoyed twenty-four-hour concierge service plus a five-star restaurant.

From what I'd found on the internet, the slips here cost more money per month than some people made in a year, and I couldn't tell if I was jealous because my dad and I always struggled financially, or if I was hating on the place because Victor lived here. *Must be evil if they'd have him as a member, right?*

"Here we are," King said, pulling up to the curb across the street.

"How are we getting in?" I noted the tall iron fence gating the parking lot. There were also security cameras and a guard by the entrance.

"*We* are not. You are staying in the car."

I didn't know whose white SUV this was. It had been parked at the private airstrip where we landed, but unless King had rented it from some Arab prince, and it came equipped with bulletproof glass and impenetrable steel doors, I was not staying in it alone. If anything went wrong with King's plan, I'd be a sitting duck out here all by myself. I assumed he and that deadly soul of his would be busy.

"I am sorry to tell you," King said, "that it is an ordinary vehicle; however, you will be much safer here than inside with me and Victor." King got out of the car, opened the back hatch, and dug something from his duffel bag.

I twisted my body and leaned between the seats. "That isn't the deal. I get to watch him die."

"You can see his body after I kill him."

I watched King remove his dress shirt, and my throat went dry. Underneath his clothes were the endless ropes of hard muscles I remembered. His stomach was rock solid with deep grooves defining each section of his abs. *So beautiful.* When I looked at King, I forgot all about who and what he was. I just got lost in him.

"What was that?" He pulled a black T-shirt over his head.

I snapped out of my distraction. "I was about to say you're out of your mind if you think seeing his body is good enough."

"You are in no position to negotiate, Seer."

"Jeni. My fucking name is *Jeni*. And we're talking about the man who took everything from me."

He shut the back of the SUV and came around to my window. I lowered it.

King spoke with a forced calm. "He did not take everything. Your father still lives and is healthy. Be grateful for what you have, Jeni."

King was right, but once again, I couldn't help how I felt. There was a rage inside me, and it had been building my entire life. Victor was the source of that rage. *All those years, he enjoyed his life, a free man, while we suffered.*

"And since we are on the subject of your father," King added, "he *must* remove the ring I gave him so he will age normally. He is not meant to live forever, and I am certain the Seers will eventually punish you for keeping someone alive past their expiration date."

Ah yes, the ring. King never told me where he got it, but when worn, it paused aging, and it could bring a person back to life after a fatal event.

I never would've believed in that kind of hocus-pocus if I hadn't personally witnessed the ring in action. My dad had been in a terrible car accident about six months ago and was put back together with so much metal that his X-rays looked like the hardware aisle at Home Depot. The worst part was his pain and the fact I had to put grad school on the back burner to support him. That was how I ended up working in Tampa after the hurricane. No, I didn't mind getting a full-time job, but it didn't help with Dad's healing process. He was not the sort of man who wanted his daughter supporting him.

Then King came along and, as a sort of bribe to

me, gave my father the ring along with one hell of a King-mindfuck. In other words, King brainwashed Dad to forget how sick he'd been and how King had smothered him with a pillow so the ring would do its job. All Dad knew was he woke up feeling great. *New body, so yeah.*

It was the moment I truly saw King for the first time. Ruthless ruler. Unafraid of killing or death. Willing to do what no one else would if the outcome was worth it. King was an enigma, everything cold and cruel and kind all rolled into one. He was educated, well-read, and wise. But he was also so damned tainted by the world that none of it mattered.

"Judge all you like, Seer. Someday, you will have to fight, kill, and compromise everything you are to protect someone you love. You will not come out unscathed."

"I never planned to live forever anyway."

"Not to worry, nothing truly lasts forever. And my time will soon be up, which is why I will once again mention I am leaving you everything I own—money, homes, cars, books, and—"

"I don't want them."

He leaned into the window, invading my personal space. I loved and hated having him so close. He smelled amazing—like clean ocean air with a hint of old-world spices. Flowers, cinnamon, exotic herbs, and citrus.

"Why not?" he asked.

Did he really need to discuss this now? Victor was inside that marina. We came here to kill him not chat.

"Victor will not be easy to kill. Which is precisely why we must discuss my assets before I go in."

"You can't die," I pointed out.

"Not entirely true. *I* do not have the ability to end my life. That does not mean there isn't a way to break the Seers' curse. Who knows what sorts of objects Victor has in his possession?"

So, basically, King believed there were objects in this world that could break the bond anchoring his soul to me. If that happened, he would be reunited with his evil soul and free to die. *I wonder what sorts of objects can do that.*

"Regrettably, the sort I do not possess," King replied, "but I assure you I have many priceless treasures, and I want you to have them. Compensation. Not enough, I know, but it is all I can do. Victor should have been put to death long before he crossed paths with your mother. The organization I created protected him."

Dammit! Why couldn't King stick to his script and be a cutthroat asshole? Maybe then I might break his spell over me. Instead, he was showing remorse and kindness. *I hate this.*

"Hate it all you like," he said, his voice low and stern, "but take the offer."

"Thanks," I said, "but if it includes your creepy warehouse, I don't want anything to do with your estate." His warehouse was full of insane, seriously dangerous stuff—plants that watched as you walked the aisles; human heads in jars, screaming for mercy; jewelry with supernatural powers; ancient weapons; cursed antiques; and poisons of every kind.

"Do not forget my lucky rabbits' feet," King said dryly, mocking my disdain for his collection. "I make a killing on Etsy."

Haha. "I've been in your warehouse, so I'm pretty sure nothing lucky would survive in there."

"Wrong again. However," he removed himself from the window and began tucking in his shirt, "I have already destroyed any items that are too dangerous to be released in the world. Part of my penance."

Good to know. "So did you finally release the heads from their watery prisons?"

"No."

Jesus. "What are you waiting for?"

"They were rapists and human traffickers from hundreds of years ago. As far as I'm concerned, they can remain in those jars for eternity."

"On second thought, the heads are great right where they are." *Rot away, stupid heads.*

"Unfortunately, the ancient Seers have been very explicit in their instructions. I must erase my footprint from the world, so the heads will have to go. Eventually."

"I'll ask if they can make an exception," I said. "And, yes, I'll get the ring from my dad. As for

Victor—"

"He knows I am coming for him, Jeni, and if he sees an opportunity to use you as leverage to distract me, he will."

"Are you actually pretending you're worried about my safety?" I chuckled bitterly.

He shook his head. "Your choices are to stay here in the car or not stay in the car, but you are not going into the marina with me." King's expression suddenly shifted, like a switch was thrown. His pale gray eyes became menacing and cold. His jaw tightened. The air around him filled with a dark energy. It didn't scare me, I'd seen this side of him before, but it was a stark reminder of who King truly was. Dangerous.

"If I am able to safely incapacitate Victor," King said, "I will come to get you so that you may personally witness his skull being crushed. All right?"

"Does it make me a bad person for hoping your offer comes with some dismemberment, too? Maybe a little eye plucking? Testicle removal?"

King shook his head. "Your humor is beyond me."

Who said I was joking?

"If I'm not back in ten minutes, leave." He turned and strode off in his black jeans, black T-shirt, and boots, looking the part of the merciless, deadly King I knew. "Stay in the fucking car, Seer!" he called out, in one final warning.

As I watched King walk off down the street, skirting the iron fence, not one ounce of doubt or weakness in the way he carried himself, I could almost imagine him going into battle as an ancient king. Bare chested, sword strapped to his back, maybe wearing one of those short linen skirts.

Part of me would give anything to see King in his element before he became this "abomination of nature," as my people called him. But I didn't see him that way. He was a king who'd forsaken his destiny and people for the love of a woman from another time. Not that I had anything against Mia, but if anyone had defiled nature and broken the rules, it was her.

She was the person who traveled back three thousand years and met Draco Minos, king of the Minoans. She must've known there'd be consequences for their love and that it would change history. No, I didn't have details, but the ancient ones mentioned Draco had been destined to marry a powerful Seer from his time. Then, one day, Mia came out of nowhere and stole him away. The other woman went crazy and tried to kill him. From there, everything started—King's wrong turns and King turning evil.

"Hello, Jeni," said a dark voice just outside my open window.

I turned my head to see Victor Escorcia staring down at me with cold brown eyes.

Fuck. Speaking of evil…

CHAPTER SIX

"Get out of the vehicle, Jeni," said Victor, who was a tall, overweight man with thinning dark hair.

"If I don't?"

"Then I'll shoot you in the fucking head." Victor pulled a shiny silver gun from his pocket, and my mind instantly shifted to the tiny life inside me. I needed to protect it, which meant I had to get through this somehow. *Stay calm. Play smart.*

I opened my door and stepped from the car, raising my hands. I didn't really know why. I supposed it was what everyone did in the movies to prevent getting shot. A show of compliance. But I knew Victor wasn't here to let me live no matter how obedient I was.

"How did you recognize me?" I asked.

"I keep tabs on all my enemies."

"We've never met, so how can I be your enemy?" I asked.

"Before Serina died, she mentioned you were traveling with King. We did our research."

I'd met his deceased, super scary wife around

the same time I met King. She'd been looking for him for years, wanting to settle some old scores.

Victor waved the gun toward a black stretch limo parked up ahead along the curb. "Get in the back."

"What are you going to do with me?"

"I am going to shoot you in the goddamned face if you keep talking. Get. In. The. Car."

My eyes darted side to side. There was no sign of King or his deadly shadow anywhere. *Shit. Shit. Shit!* I hoped King would quickly figure out Victor was out here and not inside his yacht.

Needing to stall for time, I walked slowly, feigning a limp.

"What are you doing?" Victor growled.

"I twisted my ankle this morning. Slipped."

"Untwist it and walk faster."

I was thirty feet from his limo. "I'm going. I'm going." *Please, King. Please be listening. Victor is outside. He's making me get in a black limo. Hurry.*

If he couldn't hear me, neither could his shadow, but with our connection, wouldn't he sense something was up? Or was he too focused on getting inside Victor's yacht and killing him? *King. King! Help!*

Victor opened the rear passenger door and shoved me inside the limo. To my disgust, it was the type that had been tricked out inside, with blue lights and a massive wet bar toward the front. I imagined Victor used the limo to wine and dine women before taking them to their deaths.

Well, he's not killing me. I turned and kicked him just as he moved to get inside the car. He shifted sideways, and I missed. He lunged at me, and I kicked again, but he was fast.

Victor pounced, taking me by the hair and throwing me to the black carpeted floor.

"Get off! Help!" I yelled. That was when I noted the sadistic joy in Victor's eyes. He liked watching me scream in terror.

Instinctively I fell silent, turning off my emotions and sending them deep inside. With my mind quiet, the contents of Victor's head became clear. He was getting off on subduing me and intended to fully get off once he got me to his place nearby. A house with a wall around it. A soundproof room.

Oh Jesus. Heart pumping, adrenaline flowing, I swung my fists at Victor's face. "Help! Help!" Would anyone hear me? I had to try. I had to fight! "Help!"

Victor caught my wrists and pinned them down. The only thing I had going for me was that the car door was still open, so I continued yelling.

"Get the door for you, sir?" said a male voice just outside.

Dammit. The chauffeur. Of course Victor wasn't going to drive his own car!

A new image flashed in my head: Victor tying me down back at his place, putting a tube down my throat, and crushing my neck with his foot. He wanted to hear me wheezing through the tube as I struggled to breathe.

The man was sicker than I imagined, and this disturbed monster had taken my mother's life. It was hard to believe someone so worthless had decided how she died.

I snapped from my utterly abstract thoughts, realizing the passenger door was closing. "No. Don't close the door! Let me out!"

Slam!

I inhaled sharply. *King, King! Where the fuck are you? I'm in Victor's limo.*

"Take us to my rooms," said Victor, speaking to the driver, who slid behind the wheel.

Rooms. He's taking me to his rooms. King? King? Are you there?

I gazed into Victor's joyful eyes, knowing I had to get a hold of myself. I had to figure out a way to stay alive.

I'm a Seer. I could ask *them* for help.

I closed my eyes and forced myself to shut down. I'd never done it on command before, but without King, my sisters were the only ones I could turn to.

The ten women in their brown and blue tunics gathered around a long wooden table, drinking wine from little clay cups. Above them was a mural depicting ancient goddesses riding in chariots through the clouds. The smell of salt and sea filled the air around me, the aroma unlike anything in the modern world. The warm Mediterranean air was cleaner, crisper, and nourished my soul—if that was even possible.

Of course it was. After all, I was standing in a room on the island of Crete, thousands of years before Greece or I ever existed. Still, when I came here, it felt as real as anything in my twenty-first-century life.

I remained standing in the doorway, listening to the women speak. I didn't know all their names yet, since my visits were always short.

The woman seated closest to me, with two black braids down her back, grabbed a piece of orange fruit—a small persimmon maybe—from a bowl on the table and skillfully angled her knife around the skin. "Circe, I do not understand your lessons as of late," she said to the old woman with long silver locks, seated at the head of the table furthest from me. "They are dark and pointless."

As far as I knew, Circe was our elder, the wise woman, but not the leader. I guessed that role had been vacant for a few thousand years since King left.

"Life is dark. Sometimes pointless, too," replied Circe.

"But we have spent the entire day hearing about a little girl who fell into a ravine while searching for berries. You have told us every detail of her life—her family, the stench of the animals in her barn, the taste of her mother's cooking. You have told us everything except why we are listening to this."

Circe narrowed her silvery eyes. "Patience is a virtue, Olmana." Circe sat up straight and looked at each of the women around the long table. "Olmana feels you are all ready for the question. Does everyone agree?"

The women nodded, and I sighed with relief. *Thank God. Hurry up!* At this very moment, my body was in a stretch limo with the devil who wanted to turn me into a dark, sadistic fantasy.

"Very well. As you know, the girl is trapped. She has fallen into a ravine while out searching for berries. What should she do?" Circe looked at the woman to her left with light brown hair and a thin build.

"She should carefully examine the cliffs and plan her climb out."

Circe nodded and then looked at the next woman. "You? What do you think?"

The next woman hemmed and hawed for a moment. "The girl should attempt to gather any vegetation around her and rub two sticks together. If she were to light a fire, someone might find her."

"She has no sticks. The walls of the ravine are smooth," said Circe.

"She can yell for help," said a young brunette seated to the right of Circe.

"There is no one for miles," Circe explained.

"Yelling will do no good."

"Then it's out of her hands," I spouted, trying to rush things along. "If she's rescued, it'll be because of luck."

Everyone in the room turned their heads and glared at me.

"What?" I shrugged. "The girl can't call out to anyone, signal for help, or climb to freedom. The obvious answer is that it's not up to her now. Fate will decide what happens next."

"Jeni, there is a chair for you there, girl." Circe shifted her eyes to an empty seat across from her. Funny. Now there were eleven chairs. This place was weird. A dream, but nothing like any I'd ever had.

I walked over and sat with an impatient grumble. I wasn't here to shoot the shit about a hypothetical girl about to die. *I am a real girl about to die.*

Circe looked around the table at the many faces. "Jeni is correct. The girl must allow fate to play its hand. She must accept the outcome. In this case, the girl stays calm. She understands her life is out of her hands now. Her mindset allows her to live four days without water. And then the rains come. The girl believes it is a miracle meant to save her from thirst, until the ravine begins to flood. Once again, the girl believes she is doomed, but finds the strength to accept her fate. And at the moment she accepts, the water rises and lifts her up from the ravine. She is able to climb to safety." The old woman looked straight at me. "That is your answer, Jeni."

So this story was being told just for me? "No offense, everyone, but I'm trapped in a car with the man who murdered my mother. I *saw* what he plans to do to me. Are you saying I shouldn't fight? Are you saying I should let him torture me and just hope I live?"

"I am saying no such thing, girl," said Circe.

"Then?" I didn't get it.

"She's saying that accepting your fate is your only choice. It might change the game. If it doesn't, then it's your time to go."

I turned my head toward the young blonde standing in the doorway where I just came from. She had the most stunning large brown eyes that caught the light and shimmered and a mouth I often saw in my dreams. *King's mouth.* She was his daughter.

"Ariadna." I'd met her here and in my dreams several times.

She greeted me with a nod. "Jeni, nice to see you again. I understand my father is making good on his promises for once."

"He's trying. But I'm not sure how I can help him find redemption if I'm busy getting crushed like a grape in Victor Escorcia's limo."

"Do you believe your destiny is to die by Victor's hand?" Ariadna asked.

"No," I replied.

"If it is your fate, is there anything you can do about it?"

"Not without breaking some major rules." Like King had done by circumventing death for so long. "But I don't agree with the 'just chill' and let-some-dick-murder-me solution either."

"Understandable." Ariadna folded her arms over her chest. "It is not in our nature to sit idly by and allow another to harm us. But, Jeni, you must know we chose you for a reason. My father needs you. Your sisters need you. Our story does not end here, and yours will not end in the back of that man's car. If you had stayed calm," she said condescendingly, "and used your gifts to see, truly *see*, you would know this already. You were born with a powerful gift. Learn to use it."

"How?" There were no manuals for this, and the Seers weren't giving me much help.

"Trust yourself."

"Easier said than done." My entire life I'd thought the road looked a certain way. Now everything felt upended and chaotic. Nothing in this dark new world was what it seemed.

"You need to try," said Ariadna. "Your role in all this is very important to us. You do understand your purpose, yes?" More condescension.

What was her problem with me?

"Yes," I replied. "I know." I explained that the goal was for our people to return to the land of the living and to be ruled by our "lord," Lord King, as it was meant to be three thousand years ago.

But here was the part I didn't get: The bits and pieces of stories they'd told me in cryptic conversations like these were that he'd been destined to marry a powerful Seer from his time and rule the Minoans until his death. They were meant to have many children, who would help the world as it grew. So if the goal was to set things "right" again, then how did they plan a do-over for King? He would never love anyone but Mia.

"King's betrothed was Hagne," said Circe. "And, yes, King's union to her would have united his bloodline with ours three thousand years ago, creating something powerful enough to withstand the threats our kind faced in the future."

Hagne. Her name was Hagne. "So is that part of the new plan, too?" I hated the thought of King marrying some Seer woman. He loved Mia with everything that he was, and I loved him for it. There was no room for a third woman.

"No. Hagne is paying for her own misdeeds," Ariadna said. "But that is not your concern, Jeni. You must have faith in your role. Your life will end when it is meant to, and then you will join us at this table for good. In the meantime, be cautious of the man you are about to meet. He is not what you think. He will do everything in his power to pull you away from us."

"Man? What man?" I asked.

"Ariadna! That is against the rules. You have

said too much," barked Circe.

"Silence," Ariadna growled. "You've all made a mess of things for far too long, and I am the only one who can clean it up. We are doing this my way."

Ariadna pointed an angry finger at me. "Go back. And do not come here again on your own. I will summon you when the time is right."

I suddenly felt the room spinning, my mind being jerked back into that limo. *No! Don't send me there! I can't—*

The sound of male grunting and groaning filled my ears. The sensation of a heavy body crushing me under its weight grew increasingly painful.

Oh God. Please tell me he's not doing what I think! The groaning stopped, only to be replaced by a warm liquid coating my chest and neck, soaking the front of my shirt.

With a gasp, I opened my eyes.

A man with jaw-length black hair and deep olive skin hunched behind Victor with a bloody knife in his hand. Victor grabbed for his own throat as blood poured from a gaping wound.

"Oh shit!" I pushed myself to my elbows and scurried back a few inches, trying to put distance between us.

Victor fell sideways, gurgling his blood onto the leather seat.

"Hello, Jeni. Very nice to meet you," said the man with the knife, hovering in the limo doorway.

"Who-what-I—" I stared across the back of the dimly lit car, wondering if I recognized his face. I could only make out his high cheekbones, full lips, and intense eyes. I would never forget a glower like that. I didn't know him.

He stowed his knife in a sheath attached to his belt, bent down, and removed a small cuff with tiny blue stones from Victor's wrist. "Don't want you coming back, now do we, Victor?" The man slid the bracelet into his pocket and gazed at me with his penetrating eyes. "Tell King he needs to be more careful. He shouldn't leave something so precious unguarded."

"Who are you?" I muttered.

"A friend." He smiled with a venomous gleam, not so dissimilar to King. Except King had a streak of goodness he couldn't shake. It was why he'd failed at leading Ten Club; he hadn't been sick and twisted enough. But this guy? I detected zero goodness in him. No heart. No soul. All I sensed was a massive void. So then why did he just save me?

"What are you?" I asked.

He flashed that wicked smile again. "Pass along my message to King. Good night, little treasure." The man walked off.

Panting uncontrollably, my stomach in knots, I turned my head and looked at Victor. His eyes were vacant. He wasn't breathing.

Sonofabitch! I'd wanted him to die knowing his

death was the only good thing he'd ever done for the world. Instead, he probably died feeling confused because he'd been blindsided by some guy with a knife. What sort of punishment was that? Victor had gone out way too easily. Not that I wasn't grateful for being alive.

I pressed my hand over my lower stomach. *I'm grateful for the both of us.*

A small gurgling sound from the front of the limo caught my attention. I sat up. The chauffeur's head was tilted back at an odd angle. His neck had been sliced too.

Good. "Asshole."

I scraped myself up off the floor and sat on the seat that stretched the length of the car to catch my breath.

"What the hell is this, Seer?" King's head popped inside the limo.

About fucking time. I let out an exhausted sigh. "You were right. Victor knew we were coming."

CHAPTER SEVEN
KING

Victor was dead. And while I normally wouldn't give two fucks about a member of Ten Club being executed, this one concerned me. He'd had the means to protect himself.

How did the man Jeni described get to him so easily?

"Are you certain there was no struggle?" I asked Jeni as we drove to the resort I owned several miles down the coast. I owned many properties all around the world because when you lived for thousands of years like I had, land seemed to be the only thing that never went away. Governments could be overthrown. Civilizations could collapse and disappear. Currency lost its value. Gold and diamonds were difficult to carry around and could be stolen. But land was land no matter which century I lived in.

As long as you have the means to prevent others from claiming it. Which was where power came in. With power, a man could have anything he wanted.

Almost anything. And with the sorts of powers I had acquired over the centuries, I lived the life of a king no matter where I went. No one ruled over me.

Comical that these Seers believe the tables won't turn. Or that I would sit back and act like their obedient child. Sooner or later, I would find a way to break their latest curse: forced immortality. Death would not have me because I was not in full possession of my soul—the only part of me that could cross over.

They claimed this was a punishment for my offenses against them, but there was much more to the story. The Seers, too, had played a part.

Luckily for them, I do not give a fuck. I was the man who could find anything or anyone, and my focus was on finding a way to achieve my goal. Death.

Until then, I would play along, and ending Ten Club before I died had to be done regardless. I'd made a promise to Mia. Too little, too late, but I would keep it.

"I didn't see a struggle," Jeni finally replied, "but I passed out for a few minutes."

"Passed out? In the middle of being attacked?" *Appalling.* How would she protect herself after I was gone? Seers needed to be on their guard. Always.

"You weren't answering me, so I went for help."

Ah. Now I understood. "Did you see my daughter?" I sensed Ariadna's presence at all hours of the day, but she had not shown herself since the night I learned the truth about my inability to die.

"Yes. She asked about you," Jeni said.

I nodded. "Next time you see her, ask when these games will be over."

"Games?"

"I want a plan. Tell me what must be done and by when so I can be free." I did not plan to wait for anyone, but it was important the Seers believed they were in control.

Jeni raised a brow.

"Got something to say, Seer?"

"You can read my mind. So read it."

I did not have the energy at the moment. It had taken all of my power to summon my soul to kill Victor. To my surprise, I'd felt it fully return to me for a brief moment, and that was when my plans changed. I could not forgo the opportunity.

But could I hang onto my soul long enough to depart? I'd had to try. So I'd hopped aboard Victor's boat and sought out one of his security guards, who did not hesitate to put a bullet in my head.

"You tried to cheat?" Jeni gasped.

"I saw an opportunity to die, and I took it."

"Now I know why you or your shadow didn't answer my cries for help. Thanks a lot."

Jeni knew by now who and what I was. Why did it still surprise her when I acted in a self-serving manner?

I shook my head. *She's never going to learn.*

"Says the man who's in this situation because he

cheated his way through life," Jeni quipped.

"I cheated death. That is not the same as cheating one's way through life." I fought hard for everything I had, for every breath I took, waiting for my life to intersect with Mia's. She had been from this time, but we'd met when I was still just a man. A king. Unfortunately, an injury inflicted upon her by Hagne, a Seer who was once my betrothed, forced Mia to go home and seek medical attention. In her injured state, Mia needed help to make the leap, and the Seers gave it. For a sacrifice. She could never return to my time, and I had to stay behind. If I ever wished to see Mia again, I would have to stay alive and endure thousands of years without her. None of that had been easy. I'd almost given up several times.

"Now that Victor's dead," said Jeni, "and your plan to skip living-town didn't work, what's next?"

"We rest and tomorrow fly to Heathrow."

"Why?" Her brown eyes lit up.

"Sage, the next Ten Club member, lives north of London. She, too, will be expecting us."

"You. She'll be expecting *you*. Because I don't have a passport."

Good. Jeni was a liability anyway.

"Thanks," she grumbled.

It is the truth. "Did you not just end up abducted by Victor only to be saved by a mysterious stranger?"

"Only because you veered from the plan. You

were supposed to go in and kill Victor, not try to kill yourself."

I sometimes found Jeni's innocence and naiveté to be charming. This was not such an occasion. "I am an opportunist. You might try it sometime. I also recommend you rest." The tussle with Victor had rattled her. She looked exhausted, and the Seer light around her felt weak, as if she were being drained.

"I'm fine, King. And can't you just mindfuck the immigration agent or something so I can go with you?"

"I could. But I won't." *Drop it, Seer. I mean it.*

"No. I won't drop it. We discussed this already. I'm supposed to be with you and—"

"I do not require a babysitter, and the only reason I allowed you to come to Miami was because you begged for a front-row seat to Victor's death. It was a moment of weakness I regret." *Keep pushing me, Jeni, and I will throw you from this car.*

You don't scare me, she replied silently.

Yes, I noticed. Which made me question her sanity.

"So this is it?" she said. "We're going our separate ways now?"

"Yes." Jeni was an interference, always thinking about our night together, pushing images into my mind of our naked bodies—sweating, fucking, coming. In my defense, I'd had no recollection of Mia at the time, but I had no desire to relive the moment I bedded someone who was not my wife. Even if I fucking enjoyed it. Twice.

We pulled into the parking lot of the resort, and Jeni became unusually quiet. Even her mind was silent. *Ah, the Seer is finally learning how to block people from her thoughts. Good.* She needed to start honing her skills.

"Is there something you wish to say before I leave you?"

"The man who saved me tonight said you shouldn't leave me unguarded," Jeni finally muttered. "Then he called me 'little treasure.' What do you think he meant?"

"Obviously, it means he thinks you have value."

"But then why didn't he take me? He had the chance."

"People do not always act in ways that make sense to others. And some like to play with their food first." Victor was such a person. So were most members of Ten Club. "Whoever he is, be wary. Do not trust him."

"Is he Ten Club?"

"There are only two remaining members. One is a woman in the UK. The other is a very old man." Though his location was unknown, which was why I preferred saving him for last. It could take months to hunt him down.

"So you're not worried about this guy?" she asked and then added in her mind, *You're really running off when someone is watching me?*

"Yes." As Jeni had already pointed out, the young man saved her life. So while he might want her for some purpose, there were much bigger threats in this world. Me, for example. I saw no value in Seers anymore, with the exception of Ariadna because she was mine—the product of my love for Mia. I would give anything to undo my choices. Because of them, she'd been denied her human life before it began.

But I was a cold man with a hard, practical heart. I was in no position to wish for such things, and I could not bring her back from the dead. Not now. Not when I'd learned the consequences of fucking with these witches. But if I could, I would. *The rest of the Seers can disappear forever, for all I care.*

"Jesus, you're mean." Jeni shook her head of long brown locks.

I sensed her hatred growing for me. Excellent. Would make accepting my departure easier on her. It was only a question of time before I discovered the means to break the bond between her and my soul. She knew this, yet she still hoped I would remain here. For her.

Ludicrous. The only other thing I could offer Jeni in addition to my honesty was my wealth. Compensation for the damage Ten Club had done to her life.

"I don't want your money, dick," Jeni said, reading my thoughts.

"That is your choice." *But it is all you will get from me. That and a room for tonight.* "I will have a key left at the front desk. Goodbye, Seer. And good luck."

I exited the vehicle and headed for the hotel lobby.

Jeni! My name is Jeni, asshole! she screamed silently.

I smiled. Her feistiness never ceased to amuse me. I would miss it.

CHAPTER EIGHT
JENI

I couldn't believe King was about to run off to the UK, leaving me behind while some man was out there watching me.

Then again, maybe it was for the best. Sooner or later, I'd have to learn to defend myself. Me and my baby. I already felt her light growing stronger, which would make her impossible to hide from King. Not that I knew what he would do if he found out.

Probably give me one of those stone-cold stares and shrug his broad shoulders. Maybe he'd throw more money at me. King liked doing that. Made him feel all powerful and mighty.

He'd already given me some cash because I'd lost my job after he showed up at the port, demanding I help him figure out who he was. He'd had no memory.

All in the past now, but I'd had the mortgage due at the time, and I wasn't going to leave my dad homeless.

Now Dad was back to work, and we had a little

money socked away, so I didn't need King's charity.

As for King's "kingdom," which he'd offered up, I wouldn't touch it with a thousand-mile pole. It was tainted by blood, probably cursed and haunted, too.

A shiver rolled through me, thinking about being in his house in San Francisco. I'd been there a few times before he sold it recently. There'd been so many souls trapped inside that the ground sucked the warmth from my body. Everything tied to that old Victorian was hungry for light and warmth.

Then there was the basement. *God, the fucking basement.*

How many people had died down there by King's hands? Sure, they'd been his enemies, but the things he'd done to them. The way he'd made them suffer.

I shook my head, thinking about it. *The poor new homeowners. Hope they have a good exorcist.*

As for me, it was time to rally and face my biggest fear: being left to fend for myself. To some, it came naturally. But not for me. I'd lived most of my life hiding under a rock, avoiding conflict at all costs. *That was before. This is now.*

I exited the SUV, grabbed my suitcase from the back, and entered the lobby. I couldn't see much since it was nighttime, but the property reminded me of those 1950s Hollywood resorts. Palm trees, bungalows, and a private beach club. Inside the lobby, the tile floors were a sparkly gold, and the furniture was salmon with aqua accents. Totally retro.

I walked up to the reception desk. "Hi, I'm Jeni Arnold. There's supposed to be a key—"

"Ah yes." The woman, who wore her blonde hair in an immaculate bun, slid a keycard across the counter. "You have the king suite. Would you like help with your luggage, ma'am?"

The king suite. He's such a narcissist. And why put me up there? Maybe he wanted to compensate me again, this time for leaving me behind. "Um. No. I can manage."

The woman's eyes focused on the neck of my shirt. *Crap.* I really should have changed before coming inside. I was covered in partially dried blood.

"I had a nosebleed earlier," I said.

"Let us know if you need anything laundered." She smiled politely. "Also, our kitchen has switched to the late-night menu, but call down here if you want anything special. We will have it prepared and brought up to your room."

"Thank you."

"It is our pleasure, Miss Arnold. Oh, and Mr. Minos wanted me to inform you the suite is yours for as many days as you like. No charge, of course. And we will arrange for a car if you need one or for your flight home. His jet is on standby."

Mr. Minos. King had used his original last name. I guessed it struck me as odd. Weirder yet was that he'd given the staff instructions to take care of me.

See. This was why I hated him. *I don't care about you, Jeni,* I mocked his voice in my head. *Oh, here, let me take care of you. No. Wait. Go away! But do it in comfort, woman!*

"Thank you. I'll let you know if I need anything." I smiled tightly and grabbed the handle of my suitcase.

"The suite is straight through those doors, past the pool, and to the right. You can't miss it," she said. "It's the only two-story bungalow on the property."

Why wasn't I shocked that King's "bungalow" was really a two-story beach house?

I nodded my thanks and headed outside toward the pool. The resort was incredible. I wondered if that was why King wanted to give me the VIP treatment. *Let her get a taste of what I'm offering.* His kingdom wasn't all nasty heads in jars and evil trinkets.

I followed the walkway until it ended. To the right was a two-story structure with a wraparound balcony overlooking a cliff and the ocean. That had to be it.

I walked up to the heavy wooden door where a plaque read, "The King Suite."

This guy… I shook my head, pushed the keycard into the slot, and froze. *Someone's watching.* Their thoughts circled the air around me like a pack of hungry wolves out for the kill.

My heart jumped, and I swiveled on my heel, scanning the manicured tropical landscaping. Beyond the dramatically lit palm trees and walkways, I saw nothing. I heard nothing. It was just me, the night, and the waves crashing down on the beach somewhere below the bungalow.

"Hello? Is anyone there?" I said along with every woman about to die in every horror film created. But I wasn't some helpless creature, now was I? Even King believed I didn't need him to defend myself.

Maybe he was right. *See who's there. See the threat,* I told myself and closed my eyes. I visualized making my mind into an enormous bubble and pushed it into the space around me.

How the hell did I know how to do this? No one had taught me, but it felt like second nature.

After a few moments, I came up empty. Maybe because my stomach was gurgling, and I knew starving myself wasn't good. Not for the baby. Not for me.

I slipped inside the bungalow and locked the door. The air around me felt clean and light. The energy immediately cocooned me in a veil, making me feel safe.

Bastard. I hated his games. This was why he'd put me up here. The place was warded. No one could come inside and hurt me. I could rest. I could think about my next moves. I might even be able to practice my gifts without someone attacking. *Why, King? Why not tell me?*

Like I said, King was a puzzle—pushing me away while ensuring I wouldn't be a victim to this fucked-up world I knew nothing about. He wanted to give me a chance to survive, even if he hated Seers. All but Ariadna.

I flipped on the light switch next to the door, and the place lit up like a showroom.

Wow. Modern white furniture, gleaming white marble floors, and just beyond the living room, an enclosed patio with a private pool all lit up for a nighttime swim.

Okay. Maybe I could accept King's charity. At least for a few days.

This was a beautiful, safe place, and I had a lot to unpack. Victor was dead. I was pregnant. King had left me to fend for myself.

I walked over to the phone on the end table by the couch and hit the button for reception. "Hi. I'd like a really big pepperoni pizza." I placed my hand on my stomach. "And a giant spinach salad. Thank you."

Tonight I would eat and rest. Tomorrow I'd have to make a plan.

"Jeni, my little treasure, come outside. Let's not waste this time together," hummed a deep, velvety voice in my ear. "There are secrets to share and sunrises to be seen."

My eyes snapped open, and I was greeted by an unfamiliar room. *Desk. Balcony. King-size bed.* I slammed my eyes shut and reopened them.

I'm in Miami. But that didn't explain what woke me up.

I propped myself on my elbows, wondering if the rich, masculine voice I'd just heard had been a dream. "Hello? Anyone there?"

"Come and join me on the balcony."

I knew that voice. It belonged to the man who showed up in Victor's limo.

"No need to fear me, Jeni. I saved you. Remember?"

"What do you want?"

"What if I begin with the things I don't want? I don't wish to hurt you. I don't wish to scare you."

Rule number one: When someone said they didn't want to hurt you, they usually did. "So why are you asking me to leave the safety of my room in the middle of the night?" Also, the guy was on my balcony. Second floor. Not exactly a good sign.

"If you feel safer in there," he said, "I am fine with that, but the sun will rise soon, and I don't have much time."

"You're a fucking vampire?"

A hearty, deep chuckle erupted outside. "I suppose. Except I don't drink blood, I love the sun, and I can't make anyone become like me by giving them my blood."

"Sounds nothing like a vampire."

"It takes a lot to kill me, so there's that."

"Cool. Good for you. But I have no interest in talking."

"I saved your life tonight. Doesn't that deserve a few moments of your time, Jeni?"

Unsure if I'd left the sliding glass door unlocked before bed, I got up and tiptoed over to the door.

What the fuck? It *was* locked. And shut. How did his voice sound like it was right here in the room?

"Jeni? May I get on with this, or are you going to continue rummaging around inside there?"

"What do you want?" I backed away from the glass. I didn't know what he was capable of.

"A fair trade. Nothing more."

I highly doubted it. This guy had sketchy written all over him. He'd killed a powerful Ten Club member—one whom King himself had doubts about confronting. "If you're looking for a trade, I can recommend plenty of websites. Ever heard of Craig's List?"

"What I'm after can't be found that easily."

"Thus the reason I just asked what you want, asshole."

He chuckled. I guessed my crassness amused him. "I want you, Jeni."

Me? For what? Actually, I didn't care. I wanted him to leave. "Thank you. Not interested. You can go now."

"What if I said King is in danger?"

I swallowed hard. "Then I'd ask you to elaborate."

"Let's speak face-to-face."

"Why?" He had to know I was protected in here. Otherwise, he would have entered.

"Because you will not believe me unless you look me in the eyes."

I reached for the curtain and pulled it back. There stood a man dressed in black, looking surreally beautiful under the moonlit night with his high cheekbones and full lips. Yep, it was him—the same guy who saved my ass in Victor's limo.

"Who are you?" I asked.

He dipped his head of shiny dark hair. "The name is Ansin."

Red flag right there. Any man with the word *sin* in his name was trouble. "And what are you?"

"That's a very complicated question. What if I just say I come from a very old, very powerful family, and I am the last."

"I'm sorry to hear that." But why was this my problem?

"Don't be sorry. I accepted my fate long ago."

"And what do you want with me?"

"Another complicated question, but clearly you want to cut to the chase. In short, my mother was not so dissimilar to you. She saw things. Sometimes it was the future. Sometimes she saw alternate fates play out."

"So she was a Seer?"

"No. Once upon a time, there were many groups of people who had powers similar to the Seers. And like my people, most were wiped out as empires sought to conquer new territories. Our bloodline was extinguished by the Romans. You may have heard of them?"

He'd clearly made it out alive. "How old are you exactly?"

"Old enough to know my age is a number I shouldn't share." He shrugged his broad shoulders. "Tends to frighten most."

I wasn't most. "If your people were so skilled, why didn't they know the Romans were going to attack?"

"They caught us off guard. They claimed to be passing through our village in pursuit of some unruly types who'd attacked them. Our elder made the mistake of warning one of the soldiers about his health. He was unwell and would fall ill that night. Little did we know they'd take the kindness as a threat. They thought we were pagans. True by their standards, I guess. In either case, they left. Weeks went by, and then they returned one night, killing everyone except me and my mother, who was injured during our escape. She died the next day."

How sad. I knew what it was like to lose a parent. "Okay, so, what do you want from me?"

"Before my mother passed, she placed a sort

of...*curse*. On me specifically. I became the insurance policy for our people. I would live on, carrying our knowledge, our skills, and our entire history. I want to finally fulfill her wishes." He dipped his head. "With you."

I frowned, my mind attempting to sew the threads of his story together. "Wait. You're not—"

"I wish to marry you. Impregnate you. Merge our bloodlines. You are the only living Seer. I am the only living person of my people. It makes sense."

Joke is on him because I'm already preg—wait. Oh no. My pulse accelerated with panic. I didn't trust this man. He was crazy enough to show up in the middle of the night and basically ask to knock me up. If I said no, what would he do? If he found out I already had a baby inside me, would he hurt it?

I buckled down and buried my feelings. I didn't know this guy, but from the little I'd seen, he wasn't without powers. I didn't want him getting inside my head or sensing I had something to protect.

"I'm sorry," I flashed a smile through the glass, "but while that is one mighty fine offer, I'm not interested. I also don't see what this has to do with King." He'd gotten me to listen by telling me King was in danger—not likely.

"A man such as myself doesn't get this age without knowing how the game's played, Jeni."

"What game?" I frowned.

"You have something I want. And I always get what I want."

"Sorry to disappoint you but—"

"I am the danger to King. Agree to my terms, and I'll spare his life. It's that simple." He added, "Or I kill him and lock you up until you change your mind. Which you will."

I stepped back. "How can you be so sure—"

He tapped the side of his head. "In my clan, males and females carry the gene. I see you, Jeni, with a swollen stomach. I see you giving birth."

He might have the gift of sight, but he was seeing me carrying King's baby. Not his. "You need to leave now." I closed the curtains, my heart racing all over the place.

"King's about to confront a woman named Sage. She's very powerful, but he'll probably manage to execute her anyway. Then he'll begin tracking the final Ten Club member. When he comes for me, Jeni, I'll kill him. Unless you agree to my terms."

Ansin was the third Ten Club member? But King'd said the man was old and…

Oh. I guess King was right. King probably wasn't aware that the guy'd had a makeover. Ansin didn't look a day over thirty, not that I'd actually seen his face yet. Just shadows and shapes.

As for King dying, it was what he wanted. The sooner the better. He had no interest in serving as Lord King to my people, even if it was the only way to undo the damage he'd left behind by forming Ten Club.

The problem for me was that I didn't want to

lose King. I wasn't ready. Yet, because of my love for him, I also wanted his suffering to end. I was caught in an impossible situation.

"I'll leave my business card on the table out here. I'll expect your answer in two days' time. And, Jeni? I foresee you saying yes to my terms. Otherwise, I wouldn't have come and made the offer. You *will* agree to be my wife. You *will* be happy. And you Seers will get to keep your King and put him under your thumb like you've always wanted. That's what I see, and I've never been wrong. Not in two thousand years."

But the ancient ones had told me they wanted King to take his place on the throne, to lead them. On the other hand, that never made sense. From the beginning, I'd been asking why they would put him in charge—the man who'd wiped them off the face of the earth.

I had no idea what to do now. I had none of the answers, but all of the questions.

More importantly, I didn't know whom to trust.

Was I being played by the Seers? Was I being played by this guy? And what would he do if he found out there was a more powerful Seer inside me?

Would he try to take her?

Ansin was thousands of years old and looking for a woman to match his skills in order to revive his tribe. Me.

But what stopped him from changing course and taking my daughter instead? *Wait it out until she's a woman.* These were dark, sickening thoughts, but I'd be stupid not to consider them.

Fuck. I needed to talk to King before he left. I had to tell him what was going on.

CHAPTER NINE

"What do you mean Mr. Minos checked out already?" I asked the woman at the reception desk at just past three in the morning.

"He said he had a flight to catch. I'd offer to deliver a message, but we never know when he'll return."

Shit. Shit. I'd already tried his cell phone five times. He wasn't picking up. *Fucker.* He was giving me the cold shoulder.

"Thanks. Just have him call me if he happens to check back in? Tell him it's an emergency." I jotted my name and cell phone number down on a piece of paper. King had my number already, but it couldn't hurt.

"Yes, ma'am."

"Thanks." I returned to my suite and began racking my brain. I needed to find King, but how? I had no access to Ten Club records, so I didn't know where this Sage lived in the UK. King might have information in his warehouse, but that required flying back to San Francisco and finding a way into the building. The place was warded up the ass and had some of the scariest things I'd ever seen. Even King had warned me not to go poking around because he'd set traps everywhere.

I had an idea. Against my will, King had placed a mark on my wrist. A tattoo of the letter *K.* He said it would prevent Ten Club members from laying a claim on me—some ridiculous rule he'd been worried about before the night he slaughtered them. Most of them. Either way, I'd had luck before, connecting with him by touching the tattoo.

I rotated my arm and covered the *K* with my palm. A white room popped in my head. Why a white room?

I tried again and again, but nothing happened. Absolutely nothing. *Dammit!*

My only choice was to reach out to the Seers, but that wasn't a great option either. Ariadna'd scolded me for showing up last time, and now I was wondering if they'd been completely honest with me. Was this whole thing really all about turning the tables on King so they could use *him* this time around?

It made more sense than the bullshit they'd fed me.

Still, I needed to talk to King.

I had to ask the Seers to find him. *I'll go directly to Circe.*

I got into bed and closed my eyes, relaxing my body. I focused on where I wanted to go and let my mind take me.

The cobalt blue ocean roared behind me, its powerful waves crashing onto pristine white sand on a day that was too sunny to be true.

So beautiful. I stared up at the brightest blue sky I'd ever seen, wondering if this was really what Crete looked like thousands of years ago.

"Jeni, you have returned." Circe, the old woman with long silver hair, walked up in a blue tunic.

"I needed to see you."

"Ariadna will not be pleased."

And? "Why does she get a say?"

"You are asking if she is our leader?"

I nodded.

"Ariadna holds the cards to our survival, so I suppose she is a leader of sorts."

Interesting. "I know what she said about not coming back uninvited, but I need help, and there was nowhere else to go. I have to talk to King, but I don't know where he is. Can you help?"

"Did you not try to locate him yourself?" she asked.

"I don't know how." I felt a little stupid.

"Jeni, there are certain things that must be taught to a new Seer, but exploring your gifts is not one of them. Do not be afraid to use what you have."

"Here's the thing; you all assume I even know what Seers are. So we see stuff. Okay. And some can time travel, read people's minds, or track stuff down. Got it. But I don't know how it works or where my gifts come from."

"I'm sorry, Jeni, but there is no instruction book for being a Seer. Each must discover their unique gifts and master them out in the world. You have a strong ability to see the truth, so turn it on yourself. If you cannot, it means you are not ready."

So, basically, the Seers didn't want to help me because I was supposed to help myself, and that would only happen when I was ready?

"This is stupid," I said. "I don't want to go through life feeling like I'm a jack-in-the-box, waiting for something to pop out. It's also stupid that you guys refuse to help me—like my suffering is some rite of passage."

"But it is. And when you've lived, learned, and accomplished all you can in that life, you will be given another. Here. With us."

"I don't even want to be a Seer. I wish I were born normal." So far it had only brought trouble.

"Never say that, Jeni. Never think that. You are powerful—more powerful than you know, and the universe is always listening. The gods are always listening. Your wish just might be granted, and then what? Do you want to end up like Mia?"

"You mean resting peacefully?"

"You think she is truly at peace, separated from

her people?"

So she wasn't? "I thought she was dead. Dead dead. Crossed over."

"There are many places the dead go, Jeni. Not all find peace. That is why we are blessed as Seers. We are guaranteed a place among our sisters. We can continue to learn and evolve. We watch over our descendants and serve a purpose."

I wasn't sure that sounded good. "And if I don't want to live forever?"

"All will be revealed when you are ready. *You* are *not* ready. For the time being, you must earn your stripes and serve your purpose. You must start pushing yourself to learn the intricacies of your powers." She paused. "You will need them, Jeni. There is much work to do."

"In the meantime, while I'm figuring out the blessed nature of my ever-loving blessed gifts, I need help finding King. Some guy just showed up and said he'll kill King if I don't give myself to him and make lots of babies."

"Ah. The man Ariadna warned you of, which she should not have done. You need to learn to trust your instincts and yourself."

"You're not going to help me find King?"

"I suggest you make yourself a cup of tea and find a quiet place in your mind. The stress is bad for the baby."

So she knew. Which meant they all knew. Why did it surprise me? I guessed because they hadn't mentioned it. Seemed like a big deal.

"Goodbye, Jeni."

I blinked and found myself lying in bed, the sun peeking up over the horizon, shining through a space in the curtains.

I slugged my way through my sleepy fog and found my way downstairs. There was an assortment of teas and coffee on the kitchen counter. I went for the decaf green tea. In the fridge, I found bottled water and some champagne. No food. But why would there be? King hardly ate, and I highly doubted he was the cooking type.

I microwaved a mug of water, popped in the tea bag, and went outside to the enclosed patio. Just beyond the glass windbreak, miles of turquoise Florida water shimmered under the morning sun. I popped down on one of the lounge chairs and held my mug in my hands to keep them from shaking. Nerves. A lot was riding on getting this right.

Okay. Blank mind. Blank mind. I exhaled slowly, clearing my head of every thought except one. *Where are you, King? Show me.*

I let my mind wander, praying something would come to me. *Where are you, King?*

Nothing.

Goddammit, Jeni. Come on. Clear your head. Think of King. Reach for him. I set my mug on the ground and sat up. Maybe if I thought of us, of our connection, I'd get something. *Hell, the guy's soul is anchored to me.* I didn't control it, but the Seers had tethered us.

Come on, creepy shadow. Bring me to King.

My bones jarred against my skin, and I felt my mind soaring in the clouds, totally weightless and free. I was nothing and nowhere, spinning in the air with just my thoughts. But where was King? I needed to find him.

Like a rope had been tied around me, something pulled me back down to earth.

I found myself in a room. The walls were dark, and an oil painting of a woman in a big lacy dress hung just above the fireplace. King lay in a big bed with red velvet curtains and white sheets. Where was this place?

I scanned the room, looking for some clue. Maybe an envelope or newspaper. Or—a pale arm, a woman's arm, slid across King's bare chest. I couldn't see her, though; the curtains blocked my view.

What the fuck? I jolted back into my skin, my heart pounding furiously. *That asshole. He slept with someone?* Was it the woman he meant to kill? Some side piece?

I got that King's wife was dead, and technically, he could sleep with anyone he wanted, but that meant he was full of shit. All this time, he'd been telling me how much he loved Mia, that he would do anything to cross over and be with her again. It was the reason he gave when he'd rejected me after he'd regained his memories.

And I believed him. I honestly thought he was loyal to his heart, which was his one redeeming quality.

Now I really didn't know who was playing me. The Seers? Ansin? King? My mind flashed back to what Circe had said. I had to start relying on myself for answers.

CHAPTER TEN

I spent the rest of the early morning practicing the fine art of not freaking the fuck out. Surprise! I sucked at it.

Unfortunately, it didn't matter now because I wasn't in this alone. Someone very important needed me to keep it together and figure out what to do. Was I in danger from Ansin? Should I run? Let Ansin kill King? Take Ansin's offer? Ignore everything and see what happened? People were playing me. The question was, who? All right, and why? If I wanted answers, I had to push and use my gift.

After recharging with more room service, a cheese omelet and fruit bowl, I sat down and repeated the process like before. *Relax. Let mind float. Ask a question.* This time, though, I wasn't looking for King. I was searching for answers.

I got one.

It was a flash—a moment in time—like a faint memory, but it was in the future. My future. With Ansin.

I saw myself with a baby in my arms. Ansin stood next to me, beaming down at the both of us. Even more confusing was how I looked back at him. There was love in my eyes, or at least, a substantial amount of admiration.

How's this possible? How could I feel that way in eight or nine months, after the baby came? What events would occur to drive me to want a man who, not more than twelve hours ago, said he would've taken me against my will (but since he was such a nice dude, he came with a civil offer of marriage first).

I rubbed my forehead. *I can't take this anymore.* My mind hurt. My heart hurt worse. I felt sick to my stomach, and I was absolutely sure none of it was good for my baby.

I groaned and went to the kitchen to grab a water. Ansin wanted my answer by tomorrow, but I had little to go on. Considering the gravity of everything in front of me, I had to keep pushing.

I went upstairs to the master bath and took a hot shower to soothe my nerves. I wasn't showing yet, of course, but my body felt bloated, and my breasts were tender. Both made the inevitability of this pregnancy a thousand times more real. My needs were quickly fading into the background.

I dressed in a pair of sweats and my favorite pink T-shirt and got back to work.

I sat on the couch in the living room and closed my eyes, my body revving up with tingles and heat.

My heart rate slowed to a calm, steady rhythm.

"Show me, Jeni," I said to myself. "Show me the answers. What am I missing? Who do I trust if I want to survive?" I pressed my hand to my stomach, thinking about how much depended on the answer.

The face of Ariadna popped in my mind. It was her, only…smaller. Much smaller. Maybe one or two years old. I recognized her lips (just like King's), and I would know her stunning brown eyes anywhere—the way they caught the light wasn't like anything I'd ever seen.

Why am I seeing her?

Unlike the past few times, when I attempted to use my gifts and got spooked, I didn't pull back. I pushed harder.

Why am I seeing her? What is her place in all this? Show me, Jeni. Fucking show me. The image of the infant in my arms flashed in my head again. And like before, Ansin stood by my side, beaming lovingly at us.

I looked down at the face of the baby.

My eyes flew open. *No. How can it be?*

Feeling sick, I ran to the bathroom just off the living room and hovered over the toilet. My breakfast wanted to come up, but I forced it to stay down. For her. For the baby who needed me to take care of myself and happened to look like the infant version of Ariadna.

How is this happening? How could the baby in my arms look like her? But she had. The similarity was too big to ignore.

I went to the sink and splashed cold water on my face. If my vision was true, in eight months, I would give birth to the reincarnation of King and Mia's daughter.

Shit! Seriously?

I lifted my head, pushed the wet hair from my face, and stared at my tattered reflection. *The same father. King is her father.* And my blood was the same as Mia's. Seer blood.

My stomach roiled, and a wave of chills rolled through my body. I always knew meeting King hadn't been a coincidence.

Suddenly, I couldn't see my reflection anymore. I saw a pawn in a bigger scheme. The Seers were planning a comeback. That was absolutely true. But maybe this time they intended to be reborn. All of them.

And Ariadna will be the first. She'd be my daughter.

I broke out in sobs. It was bad enough knowing King loved someone else, but now I was carrying his and Mia's daughter? Circe had said Ariadna was the key to their survival. That meant Ariadna would serve some purpose or do something special for our kind.

Like, maybe being reborn and later giving birth to other Seers? Or maybe she'd ensure our sisters were brought back to this world in Seer bodies? There could be people out there with the gene, right?

I mean, just because I'm the only one alive doesn't mean I'm the last. King once told me the Seer gene skipped generations and only expressed itself in females.

No. This still doesn't make sense. Ariadna wasn't going to sniff out people with the Seer gene and orchestrate mass pregnancies. Ridiculous.

So what is her role? Why will she be the first reborn? Pushing back the tears, I closed my eyes. *See the truth, Jeni. See the truth…*

One word popped into my head: Mia.

Mia? According to King, she'd been one of the most powerful Seers ever to exist. Proof being, King had met her when she traveled back to his time, which I gathered was a very rare gift.

Wait. Circe said Ariadna was special, too. My heart crashed to my stomach.

Could I be right? If Ariadna was special like her mother, then I could only think of one reason to go through so much effort to have her be reborn first.

They want her to use her gift. They're planning something. I mean, why not have Circe go first? She was an elder, and everyone looked up to her. But no. Ariadna was coming back.

Christ. How had I not seen something strange was going on? A) The Seers bound King's soul to mine. Me, the only living Seer, who didn't have a clue how to use her gifts. No foresight. No ability to sniff out their plan.

B) They made sure King couldn't die and that

he and I would meet. Hurricane Mia brough him to me. *Mia! What are the odds?*

C) King came to me with no memory of Mia, which removed a very big obstacle to getting me pregnant. How they knew I would fall in love with him and feel such a deep connection, I didn't know, but they knew.

Add those three things together—my inability to see, King with no memory, and my feelings for him—and they enabled events to play out in such a way that I'd end up pregnant. With Ariadna. *A time traveler just like her mother.*

The pieces fit. The Seers wanted Ariadna to go back in time, and if I were to bet what the task entailed, I'd put my money on stopping it all from happening. All three thousand years of King. It was the only logical explanation.

The Seers said that King had to fulfill his destiny in order to make things right. He'd been destined to marry Hagne, a powerful Seer from his time, not Mia. And that one event triggered three thousand years of damage to the world because King had gone on to cross many paths, alter many lives, and create Ten Club.

Ariadna is going to stop her mother from meeting King—or Draco Minos. That has to be their plan.

I slammed my fist on the bathroom counter. "Idiot! Jeni!" I knew the Seers' stories hadn't been making sense, but I'd been so caught up inside my own head, I couldn't see any of it. There was no possible way for King to make "everything right" just by killing off a few Ten Club members and doing a few good deeds. No way. Ten Club had left a massive scar on the world. They'd impacted thousands of lives and families. King couldn't atone for that.

To make things right, King had to go back to the very beginning and do it right this time.

But what about Ariadna? If King never fell in love with Mia, Ariadna would be giving up her life. She wouldn't be born.

My stomach squeezed into a tight knot. Maybe that was why Ariadna got pissy with me. She was about to give up everything for our people.

So what did this mean for me?

If Ten Club was never created, Victor Escorcia probably would have gone to jail long before he crossed paths with Mom. She might still be here today. Dad would be a completely different man with a different life. A happy one.

Who wouldn't want that? Except... My eyes teared up again, realizing if the Seers went through with this plan, I would never meet King. He'd die, as he was meant to, thousands of years ago. He'd be nothing more to me than a footnote in one of the hundreds of history books I'd read.

I circled my hand over my stomach. No King meant no baby. Not this one, anyway.

I slowly walked to the living room and sank back down on the couch. I felt like I'd been hit in the heart with a three-thousand-year-old sledge-hammer.

Everyone had been lying to me. King, the Seers, Ariadna. Everyone except Ansin. How ironic since he was a Ten Club member, and the Seers had warned me to steer clear of him.

They probably just didn't want him getting in the way of their plans. Ten Club members were notorious collectors of people and objects with power. Ensuring King killed the three remaining members, Ansin being one of them, would help keep Ariadna safe until she was ready to carry out her task.

In fact, now that I thought about it, King would never have stayed for me. But for his daughter? Of course he'd stay. It would be what Mia would want because King was powerful and ruthless. He would be the protective father Ariadna needed until her destiny came calling.

That's what this "penance" crap is all about. The Seers wanted King to do some cleanup and then protect Ariadna. The rest of their story, about him paying penance and "erasing his footsteps," was bullshit. Sort of. They really did want that to happen, but King had no idea his role would be guarding the only person capable of making it happen. A new reality.

That new reality would include King taking his place as the Seer lord three thousand years ago, as he was meant to do.

I whooshed out a breath and threw my head back on the sofa. *I can't believe this.* The pieces fit so neatly together that if it weren't for my Seer abilities, I would be calling myself crazy. But I had no reason to doubt the visions I'd seen and what I felt.

The question was, now that I knew the truth, what would I do?

Once again, I was the girl with all the questions and none of the answers.

CHAPTER ELEVEN

After hitting a dead end, I decided it was time to go home to Tallahassee. Dad had no clue about any of the crap going on, but he was the only person I trusted now.

Would he believe me? Or would he nod reassuringly while secretly thinking his daughter had lost her shit? I prayed for the former, because I had to make a choice. An important one.

Letting things play out as the Seers intended meant having a baby and raising her and loving her and protecting her, while knowing she would eventually leave me. I would forget her the moment a new reality took hold. Or worse, maybe I would remember her, like a dream that never happened, and miss her all the same. Letting things play out meant King would have to stick around to protect Ariadna, but he'd remain madly in love with Mia. I would have to endure years and years of those looks—the ones he gave when he was wishing she were here instead of me. The Seers' plan meant they had no intention of allowing Ansin to kill King—

because why take away Ariadna's protector, right? Which meant Ansin would be the one to die if the two went head-to-head, and I'd never know why I looked so happy in my vision with Ansin. And, finally, their plan also meant growing up with Mom alive—one more reason I wanted to talk to Dad. What would he say when I told him I had the power to erase the past and bring back the love of his life?

The other option was to stop the Seers' plan from happening. The most obvious choice was to raise the baby to see that her future wasn't fixed. My daughter could say no to the Seers and live *her* life. Not the Seers'. Not mine or King's, but hers.

As for King, I could hide the truth and say nothing about Ariadna. He'd have no reason to stay. In fact, if I told him Ansin planned to kill him, King would probably respond with, "Yes, please! I'd love to die." Provided that Ansin could actually end a man who kept coming back, King would get what he wanted, my heart would be broken, and the world would remain as is. The damage done by Ten Club would be a permanent fixture in a corrupt and angry world.

Not that I believed evil existed solely because Ten Club was created. It was like King had said: evil would always exist. But this? Ten Club was a cancer.

In short, my options were to stop the Seers or let things happen. Neither sounded great.

After a short plane ride on King's private jet, which he'd so generously left on standby for me back in Miami, I arrived to my dad's house via Uber.

Funny. Why did I say "my dad's" house? I still lived here. Officially. Maybe it didn't feel like my home anymore because I'd changed so much. A few weeks ago, I was nothing more than a little mouse everyone wanted to stomp on.

I lugged my suitcase to the front door of our dark green ranch-style home with neatly pruned trees and a freshly mowed lawn. It was wonderful to have the house like this again. For months after Dad's accident, the yard was a nightmare of weeds. Inside hadn't been much better. But with Dad laid up and me working all the time, cleaning and yardwork had taken a back seat. Now everything looked spotless and cheery. It felt good having Dad back, living life and driving trucks again. Work was important to him.

"Dad? Where're you? I'm home!" He was supposed to be off on Sundays.

"Jeni, that you?" he called out. "In my bedroom!"

I followed the short hallway past my small room, where I parked my suitcase and purse, before entering the master. My father was doing arm curls in the mirror by the closet, his sandy blond hair all sweaty.

I tried not to laugh. "Hey. What's going on?"

"Ah. Trying to get a little muscle tone. Impress the ladies, yanno? Watcha doing home so early?"

I'd lied and told him I'd taken a temp job in San Francisco for a few weeks because my boyfriend, King, was considering relocating. I wanted to try the city on for size.

I sat on Dad's springy queen-size bed. "Actually, I came home because I need to talk."

"Uh-oh. I know that look, Jeni. Something's wrong." His light brown eyes went wide, and he set the dumbbell on the floor. "You're pregnant, aren't you?"

Damn, Dad. Can't you let me work up to that? With a sigh, I looked down at the floor. "Yes, but—"

"Jeni!" Dad darted over and leaned down, wrapping his arms around my shoulders. "I knew you and King were a good fit. The way he looked at you—I know love when I see it." He let me go.

King did *not* love me. But when Dad had met him, King still had no recollection of Mia. Whatever desire he'd felt for me then was long dead now, never to be resurrected. Unlike him.

"He's not in love with me, Dad. That's why I'm here." I exhaled sharply, dreading this conversation. "I need your advice."

Dad sat next to me on the bed. "You're not thinking of getting rid of the baby, are you?"

"No. Not at all." I placed one hand protectively over my stomach.

"Good. Because I've always wanted to be a grandfather, so if you're worried about support, I'm here for you. Whatever you need."

God, I so loved that about him. It was why he and my mother had been inseparable. Two peas in a pod. They were "give until it hurts" kind of people.

My eyes teared up. I seemed to be doing that a lot lately. Hormones. "Thank you, and you know I'm here for you, too."

Dad took my hand, and that was when I saw the gold ring. *He's still wearing it.* Another reason for me to dread this discussion.

The ring used to belong to King, but he'd given it to Dad in order to heal him. An act of goodwill toward me when King needed my help.

Dad remembered none of the details, because King had put the whammy on him—told him he'd had a bad accident and was all better now. But how would my dad react when I told him the truth? While I slept completely unaware in the other room, King had smothered my dad with a pillow. That was how the ring worked. You wore it, you didn't age. If you happened to croak, it would bring you back in a shiny new body. This "man" my dad loved so much for me had, without hesitation, snuffed out his life to prove himself.

"Dad, I have so much to tell you. But before I start, I want you to promise two things."

"Okay." His brows pulled together.

"Keep an open mind, and don't have me committed."

"Jeni, what's wrong?" His voice was saturated with worry.

"Everything. Everything's wrong. And the problem is, I'm not so sure if I should change it." That was the question, right? Do nothing. Or fight to keep everything the same. Total insanity.

"I've never seen you like this. What's going on? If King hurt you, I'll kill him."

King hurt me all right. But not the way Dad thought. It was way more twisted than anyone could imagine.

I drew a slow breath. "This is the part where you have to keep an open mind, Dad. And listen. Just listen."

About an hour later, I'd told Dad the short version of my completely unbelievable story. What worried me most was how he sat afterward, staring at the wall.

"Dad? Say something. Say I'm crazy. Say you love me even if I am crazy. Say—"

"I need a drink." He got up and left the room.

I whooshed out a breath and followed him to the kitchen, where he emptied a quarter bottle of whisky into a coffee mug—probably because it was the closest thing in reach.

"Dad? Talk to me."

He gulped down his drink and set the mug on the white tile counter. "Do you trust them?"

"Trust who?"

He turned to face me and leaned against the counter. "Do you trust these…*witches*? These Seer women?"

My mouth flapped for a moment. "I-I don't know. Why?"

"Because you'd have to if you let them reset three thousand years of history. You'd have to be one hundred percent certain that the world will be better off. Not just for them, but for all of us."

"So you believe me?" This wasn't the response I expected. Was he for real? Or was he appeasing me and planning to call the crazy-bus to come get me after I left the room?

He hung his head. "All I know is that my daughter is the most loyal, honest, and hardworking person I've ever met. I know she's the best of both her parents. I know I can't trust much in this world, but I can trust you."

My eyes filled with tears. I didn't want to cry. Not now. Not when I needed to keep a firm grip on my emotions. "Thank you, but…you really believe me?"

"I don't have to believe. I trust you. And if you're saying you're some sort of witch and your boyfriend is a ghost… Well, as impossible as that sounds, I have no reason to doubt you."

"I'm touched, but I'm not a witch. And King isn't a ghost. He's…" I wasn't sure what he was. A dead king who couldn't die, who couldn't live. He was what he was. King.

Dad stepped forward and took my hand. "I remember, Jeni. Not everything, but bits and pieces from after my accident. I wanted to discount them as dreams because I'd gone through so much pain, but now, hearing your story, I know it's true. I know King did something to me."

I bobbed my head, my lower lip quivering. *He believes me. He believes me.* It was a huge relief. "So what do I do?"

He dropped my hand. "Like I said: Do you trust these women? Seems to me they market themselves as healers and saints, out to save the world, but if that were true, then why did they plan to take over this Ten Club? Why slaughter King's pregnant wife? Why kill his infant son? Why not just," he shrugged, "let them live and punish King instead?"

That was a very, very good question.

He continued, "I know I don't have a degree in history like you, but I've read enough to know there's a pattern with tyrants throughout history: They market themselves as saviors. But at the end of the day, no one good, *truly* good, would want to take over a supernatural billionaire club or rewrite history unless they were after power."

Dad was right. And not just right but fucking right. All along I'd bought into the notion that the Seers were good. All of them. But what if they weren't? What if they were just people? Good. Bad. Somewhere in between. It was like King said: *"Seers are no different than anyone else with the exception of their abilities. They must choose which path they take in life."*

"You could be right," I admitted. "But I can't argue with their point: King outlived his normal lifespan by thousands of years and created this monster, all because he claims it was the only way to keep control over evil people."

"Who's to say he isn't right, Jeni? Power and greed are the sickness of every generation. Look at the Maya. Look at the Egyptians. They weren't the nicest people. They enslaved other tribes, murdered in tribute to their gods, and performed unspeakable acts. You don't know what the world would look like today if King hadn't chosen to become king of the wicked in order to contain them."

"You honestly think he did the right thing?" I scoffed.

"I'm saying we don't know anything except for this outcome—what we see here and now. The rest is a guessing game for everyone except those Seers. But I think, given the nature of man, the probability that a bigger, badder fish would have taken King's place in history is very strong."

"Maybe the Seers would've filled that void," I concluded, thinking hard about how power corrupted. "What about having a different life with Mom in it?"

"I loved your mother more than anything in the world besides you. But if she were alive today, she'd probably tell you that the grass is never greener. It's our struggles that make us strong, so why would society as a whole be any different?

"Where would we be today if, for example, people hadn't fought the Civil War because it was just too ugly? Or World War II? Humankind has faced some very horrible situations, only to come out of it just a little better. Take those away, and I'm not sure the world would be a better place. Take away Ten Club, and maybe it's the same. We don't know the roles they've played."

"I never thought of it like that." He'd given me a lot to think about. Mostly, the "where would we be if it weren't for our hardships" part. What killed me was how King'd said the exact same thing: "*...every hero, every great man or woman—from the fictional god to the legendary historical figures who triumphed against all odds—had their moment of transformation. They faced the worst this world has to offer and rose like a phoenix.*"

"Darn." Dad looked at his watch. "I have a date in thirty minutes. Let me call her and cancel."

"A date? With who?" I asked, totally shocked.

"She owns the flower shop next to Target."

I'd been in there a few times buying flowers for Mom's grave—every birthday, every holiday. A pretty redhead woman ran it. Her name was Simone or Simmel or something.

Dad added, "It's actually our third date, and we're really hitting it off. She's taking me to see an exhibit with unicorn-shaped topiaries."

Strange. But okay. At least my dad was finally moving on. A good thing. Even if it made me more confused about what to do. "Don't cancel on her, Dad. I'm fine. Was going to take a nap anyway."

"You sure? Because I don't mind."

"Yes. Go. Have some fun." If anyone deserved it, he did.

Dad slid King's ring off his finger and placed it on the counter. "Tell King thank you for giving me back my life and healing me."

I nodded and folded my arms across my chest. "I'll let him know." *If I ever see him again.* That fucker was in the UK, cozying up to some woman.

"Why don't we talk more when I get back?" Dad said. "And you should get some rest. You look tired."

"Thanks." I *was* exhausted. I'd been using all my Seer juice to figure things out.

Dad left to get ready, and I started searching the cupboards for a healthy snack. Meanwhile, my mind hopped back to King. Of course it did. He was never far from my thoughts, which really bugged the shit out of me. He obviously didn't care about me, but why lie and say he only had eyes for Mia? Why fuck some random woman?

It makes no sense! He's King. Just tell the truth.

Wait. A shock wave spiked through me. I believed in King's love for his family. And being a Seer, it would be hard for him to fake that with me, wouldn't it? I could see straight into his damned heart.

So if he hadn't been lying about his feelings for his late wife, then… I pressed my hand over the *K* tattoo on my wrist. Maybe there was a reason I hadn't felt a connection with him when I touched it earlier. *Something's wrong.*

I hurried to my bedroom, shut the door, and lay on my bed. The space was still crowded with boxes piled up against one wall. I never had the chance to unpack after moving back from college because I'd jumped straight into taking care of Dad and working full time.

Okay, Jeni, I told myself, *do it just like before. Breathe and let go. Breathe and let go. Breathe and—*

My mind began to soar like a bird, flying through a dark sky. Below were large black spaces broken up by clusters of lights. Small towns or villages maybe?

Where is King? Show me King.

I felt myself falling toward the earth, passing through bricks or some sort of stone, landing in the same room as before with the red velvet curtains. Only this time, the curtains were pulled all the way back. So were the covers.

Oh God. What is this? I wanted to vomit. It was so horrible and gory that my mind couldn't process it. Not in a million years.

I jackknifed in bed, grabbed my purse, and dug out Ansin's card. I slid my cell from my pocket and dialed the number.

"Didn't expect to hear from you until tomorrow," he said, his voice deep, cocky, and thrilled, "but I'm glad you called, my little treasure. Come to a conclusion, have we?"

"I want you to help King."

A hearty chuckle erupted on the other end of the line. "Help him? I mean to kill him, Jeni—unless you're agreeing to my terms. Are you agreeing?"

"No. But I'm going to ask you to hear me out—just like you asked me to do."

"Why should I listen? What's in it for me, little treasure?"

He wanted to make a trade just to hear me out? I had nothing to give except, well, information. "What if I told you the Seers are planning to rewrite history, one without Ten Club?" He would care about that, right? Like the other members, I guessed he'd been acquiring powers, money, and skills because of them. They all traded.

"Then I'd say where do you want to meet?"

CHAPTER TWELVE
ANSIN

My little treasure is asking me for a favor? I chuckled, amused by this unforeseen twist. *Hilarious.* I was no hero. I was as coldhearted and cruel as they came. Why deny what I was? I was not here to please anyone but myself. I could admit, however, that this detour intrigued me. I had never played this role— brave knight, rescuing the damsel in distress—until Jeni came along. First I saved her from Victor, and now this.

Yes, yes. It will be fun.

I'd lived for over two thousand years, and while I had important work to do, life could get tedious, redundant. Maybe this was just the distraction I needed. A little battery recharge, if you will. At a minimum, I was intrigued. Why would a man like King require my assistance?

What happened, my little treasure? What horrors would drive you straight into the arms of a venomous snake out to bite you?

Just before ten p.m., I pulled up on my Harley

to the run-down café three hours south of Tallahassee. I'd been on my boat in Miami at the time of her call, preparing for my showdown with King. I found boats to be useful when storing things not meant for the public's eye. Or for moving items on a moment's notice.

My boat was a twenty-year-old steel trawler, complete with a crew of authentic-looking fishermen—sun-damaged faces, scarred hands, the smell of the ocean permanently infused in their skin. They looked authentic because they were authentic. In their minds, they spent their days fishing for red snapper and grouper, but really, they slept, ate, maintained the boat, and lived in a fantasy world I had created just for them.

My kind of power was useful, though I'd acquired this particular trick from Sage, the woman King was hunting at the moment. Sage had very interesting tastes in the occult, but her dream potions were the only things of value to me. She was also known for her druid tattoos. Protection wards, immortality, physical strength—she had a tattoo for everything. Made millions off them. Of course, if any of her clients ever displeased her, she had the power to sour those tattoos and turn them into painful punishments. Luckily, I never needed her help with such things. My mother had seen to my immortality and power.

Unfortunately, I was fast approaching a bottleneck. As one individual, I could only manage control over so many people and things. It was time to expand. But finding people I could trust, who would obey and use their gifts in ways that served me? Not easy.

Trust me. I'd tried.

Family were the only ones with true loyalty. Children, in particular, could be taught to do things my way.

That was where Jeni came in.

Together, she and I could have ten, eleven children. Maybe more if we pushed it. Each one would be a force all their own, and I would ensure they were raised to understand the meaning of loyalty and obedience. I would teach them to fight.

The next group of tyrants who come knocking will be greeted much differently. Had my elders been more prepared, our people would still exist. Instead, we had been wiped out by a pack of narcissistic, power-hungry Neanderthals with swords and leather skirts.

Fuck the Romans.

So, yes, there had been *some* truth to the story I gave Jeni. I wanted her for her powers. True. I wanted to resurrect my bloodline. True.

However, this time around, they would be warriors and more powerful than any battalion, Ten Club, or group of Seers. My new family would not be victims or Celtiberian pagans who held hands around a campfire and debated ad nauseum over each and every decision. They would have a strong leader. A ruthless leader. One leader. Me.

I unzipped my leather jacket and entered the café, a bell chiming my arrival. I immediately spotted Jeni sitting in a booth toward the back, with her dark hair in a messy bun.

She looks tired. I could see the bags under her eyes from here.

A waiter appeared to my side. "Good evening. How many?"

I offered him a scowl. Only pathetic, weak men waited on others. *Someone should confiscate his penis.* "Bring me a black coffee and then fuck off."

The pitiful excuse of a man blinked and walked to the coffee station.

Jeni's gaze caught mine, and I watched as her warm brown eyes drank me in.

That's right, my little treasure. This is what I look like in the light. I was the real fucking deal. Pure male.

The handful of patrons inside the establishment took notice too, straightening their backs.

Yes, motherfuckers, the big bad wolf is here. And he wants to kill, fuck, and rule over all you little bunny cunts.

The patrons looked away. Not Jeni, though. Jeni's mouth dropped open.

If I didn't know any better, I'd think it was an invitation.

My cock stirred with heat. *Soon. Not to worry. Soon.*

I walked over and slid across from her into the

booth. Her soft eyes reminded me of a sad song. Beautiful, but tormented. Her small frame with large breasts was like a river flowing with curves. *And soon to be wet.* Her long brown hair was like her heart, all knotted up, holding back her true wild self. But those lips. Those fucking lips. *Clearly they were meant for sucking cock. My cock.*

"What the hell?" Jeni gasped.

"You heard that, huh?" I flashed a wicked smile. *What can I say, little treasure? I am a man who knows what he wants, and you have a set of lips meant for more than smiling.*

"I didn't hear it. I saw the image in your head." She leaned in and hissed, "What the hell is the matter with you?"

"Everything." I continued smiling. "Now tell me what you want, my little treasure. You have two minutes." I leaned back in the booth.

Jeni reached for her coffee. "Don't play games, Ansin. You didn't drive three hours to give me two minutes." She put the mug to her mouth, and I watched in fascination as her lips touched the rim and then puckered ever so slightly as she drank.

Mmmm… "Fair enough. I'll give you five." Long enough to watch her finish her coffee. "But then I have a red-eye to catch and a king to kill."

The waiter appeared with shaking hands and my coffee and then promptly fucked off as instructed. I took a sip of the piping hot liquid and felt immediately tempted to murder whoever had brewed this shit-flavored broth. How hard was it to make a decent cup of coffee in this day and age? They had every brewing contraption known to man.

I slid my mug aside, and when I looked up, Jeni's eyes were flickering with hate. I kinda loved it.

"What?" I said.

"You're *not* going to kill King," she said.

"I'm not?" News to fucking me.

"No. Because you made an offer to spare him."

"Indeed I did, little treasure. Unfortunately, what you asked for over the phone was something different. My original offer was to spare King, and sparing a man from your sword is vastly different than pledging your sword to save him."

"Stop calling me *little treasure*. And I'm asking you to let him live. The outcome is the same."

But the task wasn't, and Jeni knew that. "Everything has a price, *little treasure*. So if I save him, what do I get in return?"

"As *I* mentioned on the phone, I'll tell you what the Seers are planning."

"Wrong. The deal was you'd tell me their plans in exchange for coming here to listen to you." Was she testing me?

She leaned back and folded her arms over her chest, the swells of her full breasts momentarily distracting me.

"I'm renegotiating," she said. "My information in exchange for you helping King."

"Forgo killing King just for the *hope* you might

give me something useful?" I shook my head and chuckled.

"To live is to risk."

She wanted a quote war, did she? "To react is for fools. To act is for victors."

"Shit or get off the pot." She narrowed her eyes.

I liked this girl. She didn't back down from what she wanted. "All right, I'll modify my original offer. I will save King if you become my wife and the mother of my children. You will also share what you know about the Seers' plans. But I have one additional stipulation: You must be obedient." I hoped she would say no. The mother of my children needed to be a fighter.

"Fuck you. I will never be obedient."

I think I just came in my leather pants. "We'll see," I said, knowing she was perfect. "So now that we've agreed, tell me what happened to King."

She looked out the plate-glass window, and her grip tightened around her coffee cup.

I waited, thoroughly intrigued.

"I-I…" Jeni's eyes began to water.

"Clock is ticking, Jeni."

"I saw King's body on a bed. He was cut open, his chest completely hollowed and his organs removed. Around the room, there were jars containing everything they'd ripped out. Heart. Lungs. Liver." She began to sob. "But there were so many jars. More than any human body could possibly contain. I think they're letting him come back to life in a new body and harvesting his organs all over again." She covered her face. "So much blood. I can't get the image out of my head."

Is that all? I tried not to react or smile. For a man like King, this was child's play. He'd dished out punishments to Ten Club members who'd broken the rules that were a thousand times crueler. *Even makes me uncomfortable.* Which said a lot.

I slid my hand across the table and patted Jeni's hand, growing irritated by her sobs. "You can stop that now. He will be fine." As my fingertips touched her, a spike of warmth surged through my hand. I pulled it away.

My, my, what was that? My little treasure was becoming more interesting by the minute.

"Sorry." Jeni reached for a napkin from the dispenser on the table. "I've just never seen anything so violent."

Again, I stifled a smile. It was almost adorable how untainted she was by this world. "Let us go now to save your king. We have a long flight."

"But I don't have a passport."

This time, I couldn't hide my amusement. "Oh, my little treasure," I chuckled my words. "How innocent you are." I slid from the booth and stood. "Passports are for those who adhere to the laws of men and believe they have to ask permission. People like us *don't* ask permission. Hurry now. I don't want to miss the flight or the next show." Sage was quite skilled with a knife. Fortunately, I was better.

CHAPTER THIRTEEN

JENI

Seeing Ansin during the day was not the same as seeing him at night when his chiseled, dark features seemed elegant and seductive.

Now I could see the golden rings around the irises of his black eyes. I could see the faded scars on his deeply tanned face that left lines on his jaw where the stubble no longer grew. I could see the fine wrinkles around his lips that, despite their fullness, looked stiff. Like he'd forgotten how to smile. Really smile.

He was hard and cold, and everything about him told me he was not to be trusted, that he was more animal than man. Even the way he carried himself—like he could kill you with one look, because he probably could—was unlike anything I'd encountered. Not even King walked like that. Then again, King tried to hide what he was. This man chose to advertise it.

"Get on." Ansin mounted his chrome and leather motorcycle.

"I'm not riding that." I was pregnant. Also, I didn't see any helmets.

"You are if you want to make our flight." He raised a black brow and pushed his jaw-length hair back behind his ears. Now I realized why he probably wore it long; his ears were scarred, too, but worse than his face, like someone had branded him with wire mesh.

I wonder what happened to him. Something told me it was a lot of somethings. Maybe the result of being alive as long as he had and not having King's ability to come back in a shiny new body?

He pumped that pedal thing with his foot, and the bike roared to life. "You coming or not, Jeni?"

The hard lines of his lips momentarily distracted me. He was a beautiful man. Or was a beautiful man once. I could see pieces of the original framework—pronounced cheekbones and a strong jaw, a square chin and deep, intense eyes—peeking through the bitterness and scars. *I bet he was breathtaking when he was younger before the world took pieces of him.*

We locked eyes for a moment, and a spike of fear charged through me, followed by adrenaline. I wasn't completely afraid of Ansin, but I certainly wasn't comfortable. One thing was for sure, Ansin liked the way I was looking at him. I could tell it gave him a subtle satisfaction. Just like when he walked into the café. The patrons nearly shit themselves, and there'd been a smugness on his face.

I drew a deep breath and got on the back of the bike.

"You're going to have to put your arms around me," he said.

I hesitated. This man had a wicked vibe that made me want to push away, but if I wanted to help King, I'd have to get through this.

I slid my arms around his torso, feeling the coolness of his leather jacket seep through my shirt into my chest. I pushed my hands through the opening of the jacket, pressed my fingertips into the soft fabric of his T-shirt. I felt his warm, hard muscles underneath.

A cold tingle rolled down my back. Everything in my body was telling me to run. He was bad. He was dangerous. And he might actually be more evil than King.

Ansin put the bike in gear, and we took off. He obeyed no speed limits. He obeyed no traffic laws. He drove like he owned this world and anyone who valued their lives should get out of his way.

They did.

And I needed to watch myself. Because, as much as he frightened me, his powers fascinated me.

Ansin was very different from King. For starters, well, King was once a king. He liked expensive suits, expensive cars, and private jets. King enjoyed the finer things money could buy. Ansin, on the other hand, didn't seem to give a shit about any of that.

When we pulled up to the airport in Miami, he parked the bike at the curb, left the keys in the ignition, and told me to follow him inside to the ticketing counters.

"Are you just going to leave your bike there?" I asked.

"Yes."

"But they'll tow it," I pointed out.

"The bike isn't mine. I took it."

What? I caught up to him as he headed for the British Airways counter, not bothering to get in line.

"You're cutting in front of all these people," I hissed.

He turned and stared me down with those gold and black eyes. "I'm two thousand years old, little treasure, and like I said, I don't ask permission."

"And apparently you steal."

"Material things are meaningless. Power is everything. Never forget that." He turned to the airline employee and asked for two tickets, first class to Heathrow. She smiled, punched in some information, and handed the tickets over. No money was exchanged.

I stood there with my jaw hanging open. "How did you do that?"

Ansin handed me my ticket. "Power, Jeni."

I followed him through security—no one asked us for a thing—and we boarded the waiting plane moments before the doors closed. He'd been right; we'd just made it on time.

"How do you make everyone just do what you want?" I asked quietly, settling into my first-class seat. It was pretty impressive, even if I didn't agree with not paying for things. It felt wrong.

"Don't tell me you've never seen King use that trick." He removed his leather jacket, exposing his tanned, extremely jacked arms, which were covered in linear scars. They looked like they'd been cut with knives repeatedly in a crisscross pattern.

Again, I wanted to ask what had happened to him, but I had a feeling he'd either tell me to fuck off or the story would be horrific.

"No. I mean, yeah," I replied to his question, "I've seen King do mind tricks, but not like you."

"Not like me, how?"

"King tries not to be noticed. He's subtle when he uses his powers in public. You seem to—"

"Not give a fuck? It's because I don't, my little treasure." He leaned back in his chair and closed his eyes, just like I'd seen King do. He was gearing up for something. "Besides, what can these people do to me that hasn't already been done?"

Now I had to ask. I couldn't resist. "What's been done to you?"

"I've died more times in more ways than you can imagine."

"I'm sorry to hear that."

"Don't be," he replied flatly. "I'm not. Now, if

you don't mind, I need to take a nap."

A nap? Men like him napped? I supposed they did, but it sounded strangely weak coming from such a dangerous SOB. Children napped. Men slept.

"Wake me when we land," he added.

"Okay, boss."

Ansin's eyes flew open. "Don't ever call me that. You are to be my wife, not my employee, slave, or servant."

My back stiffened. I'd triggered him, but why? I mean, yes, I got what he just said, but his reaction was a little over the top. "Then why did you ask me to be obedient when we were at the café?"

He closed his eyes again, and one corner of his mouth turned up into a smile. "It was a test. Now get some rest. You're going to need to be on your toes when we arrive to the castle. Sage'll have many tricks up her sleeve."

She lived in a castle? And what tricks? What were we walking into? "Care to provide details?"

Ansin's face relaxed. He was already asleep. Or maybe his mind went somewhere, like mine did when I used my powers.

Whatever the case, I needed to curb my intense curiosity about Ansin and start paying attention to my fear. He was not the type you should let your guard down around.

He was not to be trusted.

CHAPTER FOURTEEN

The eight-and-a-half-hour flight felt like an hour. I'd closed my eyes for a moment, and suddenly we were landing. I looked to the seat next to me, where Ansin was already awake, doing something on his phone.

I wondered if he actually owned the device, or he'd just walked up to someone, held out his hand, and they gave it over.

"So," I said, my voice scratchy, "what's the plan when we land? Aside from strolling through customs and stealing someone's motorcycle."

"It's raining. We'll need a car." He didn't bother looking up from his phone.

"Ah. Well, I need to eat something." My stomach was a mess. Possibly morning sickness kicking in.

"I'll grab you something on the way out."

Meaning, he would literally walk in and take food. "I don't mean to pry, but don't you have any money? A credit card? Some gold coins?"

"Yes, you do mean to pry. And yes, I have plenty of money. I'm not a fan of wasting time paying for things that mean nothing to me."

"Those things mean something to the people you're taking from."

"Those people will be dead in ten, twenty, fifty years. And trust me, I've witnessed enough people dying to tell you they won't give a fuck about their things when their time is up."

"No?" I wasn't arguing with that statement, but I did wonder what *he* thought they gave fucks about. "What will they be thinking about?"

He kept his eyes glued to his phone, typing away with his thick thumbs and strong hands. Even his fingers looked like they spent time at the gym. Or in battle.

"Time," he replied bluntly, disinterested in the conversation. "They all wish they had more time. Which is why I don't waste mine on shit that doesn't matter."

Interesting philosophy. "So where do you plan to raise this child you want me to have if you don't believe in taking the time to own things?" A purely hypothetical question because I wasn't planning to let him anywhere near me. Yes, we had a deal, but I'd find a way out of it. King would know how—something to barter for or…whatever.

"Not child. Children," he corrected. "And you do not have to worry about that. I will ensure you want for nothing."

Children? I blinked, feeling my pulse race. I definitely had to make sure King was rescued and got me out of this.

Noticing my silence, Ansin finally looked up. "Did you think I planned for my offspring and you to live in a cardboard box?"

"I have no idea what to expect from you, Ansin. You're nothing like I imagined."

His black and gold eyes flickered. "Did you imagine I'd be like that dainty, pompous King of yours?"

"He's not mine."

"But you want him to be, don't you?"

I said nothing.

"Don't worry, little treasure, nothin' worse than being thirsty. I get it. And you're in luck, because I'll never ask you to thirst for me. I just want you as my wife and to give me children."

"How romantic."

"If you want romance, I'll buy you a book. Just remember our deal. I save your precious King, and then you're mine."

I swallowed hard, thinking about what Ansin might do when he found out my body was already in use by King's baby. I had to be prepared to protect Ariadna. But how?

Focus on getting King free first. I didn't know what went wrong or how this Sage woman had subdued King, but I knew it took a lot to blindside someone like him.

"Are you afraid of this Sage person?" I asked.

Ansin cocked a black brow and gave me a look, like he was wondering if I was a moron.

"I'll take that as a no. And you can remove the

stick from your ass. It was just a question." Everyone was afraid of something. If I got lucky, I'd find out Ansin's weaknesses.

"I have a healthy respect for Sage and the powers she's amassed," he said. "So while I do not fear her, I'm no fool either. I'd prefer not to end up tied to a bed, having my organs ripped out."

"So what's your plan?"

"Do not worry, little treasure. I will keep you safe." He flashed that wicked smile.

I was learning fast. It was his only smile.

"Why bring me along, then, if I'm not going to help?"

"I want you to see when I've kept my word."

I doubted that was the reason. Ansin was all about power. He probably wanted me to witness how he operated so I'd have a healthy fear of him. *Power over me. That's what he wants.* Strange because he could make me do whatever he wanted. So why didn't he?

He went back to his phone, and I spent the remaining few minutes of the flight trying to stay calm. For a second, I was tempted to try my gift again to see what we were in for at this castle, but I couldn't bring myself to do it. Not after that bloodbath I'd witnessed in my vision. Whatever awaited us wouldn't be good.

"A chauffeured car?" I stared at the man in a suit,

holding a sign that read *Ansin Bastuli.*

"I do not enjoy driving on the opposite side of the road." Ansin shrugged and shoved a paper bag in my hands. "It's a ham and cheese sandwich and some juice."

I hadn't even seen him grab it. "Thanks."

"You can eat in the car."

Of course, because Ansin hated wasting time. The strange part about him was that when he spoke, his words were carefully chosen. Never rushed. Similar to King. When Ansin moved his body or walked, he exuded the same vibe. Controlled. Efficient. Purposeful.

I realized it was a form of nonverbal communication, a message to everyone around him. *Don't fuck with me.* He was a pit viper and proud.

Ansin and I followed the driver out of the terminal.

"What sort of name is Bastuli?" I asked.

"My people didn't believe in last names. Bastuli is the region where my tribe was from. They were Celtiberians."

I'd studied history in college, but didn't know very much about them other than they lived in what was now known as Spain. "So your people were Celts?"

"They were unprepared, which is why they're all dead."

We came up to the black car waiting outside. Funny. It wasn't raining at all. In fact, it was a sunny afternoon. Just a little chilly.

The driver opened the door for us. I noticed how he avoided eye contact with Ansin. Everyone did. It was almost like he willed them not to look. Was he ashamed of his scars?

No. Silly. Ansin wore them like badges of honor.

I glanced to Ansin at my side and whispered, "Why don't people look at you?"

"Trust me, they look," he replied in his normal speaking voice. Deep. Calm. Doesn't give a fuck.

"But then they look away."

"I find it easier to get on with my business if people are unable to remember details about me."

"So you're an immortal criminal?"

"I do what I must to achieve my goals. If it so happens to be illegal, not my problem."

I bobbed my head.

"Why so many questions, little treasure?"

"Trying to understand you. That's all."

"No. It's more than that. I see it in your eyes." He leaned closer and slowly slid a hand on my thigh. "Are you getting anxious?" he said in a low voice. "Are you thinking about what it will be like when I bed you?"

My face flushed, and to my surprise, the spot where his hand rested on my thigh felt hot too. The heat traveled up my leg and between my thighs, triggering an instant wave of goosebumps. No, I had *not* been thinking about what it would be like to sleep with him, but now I was.

I pushed his hand away, and he promptly returned it.

"What are you doing?" I asked.

"I've waited a very long time for someone like you, and I have no problem admitting how much I'm looking forward to our fucking. I'm going to make you come so hard, Jeni. You'll never be left wanting in my bed."

What? My heart raced out of control. Not because I lusted after him, but because I believed him. I believed he would make me come. I believed he'd had plenty of years to master the act of pleasing a woman. I believed he dominated in bed, too, and that was my weakness. At least now it was.

Before King, I'd slept with a few guys but never enjoyed it. It was always about them and never me. In short, the sex I'd had completely turned me off from it.

Then I'd had that night with King and finally experienced what it was like to orgasm so hard that your jaw hurt from gnashing your teeth, that your body dissolved into hard waves of pleasure. King had fucked me hard and so thoroughly, I'd been sure it was all a dream. A delicious, sinful dream I wanted to have again and again and again. How was it possible that a man could make me feel so good, so dirty, so insane with need for his body? In me. On me. Behind me.

So now, hearing Ansin talk like this, I couldn't stop my pulse from racing.

It's just the hormones. That's all. "I never said we'd be having sex. There are lots of ways to get pregnant these days."

Ansin pulled away and tilted his head back, laughing so hard his chest shook.

It was the first time I'd seen him not look, well, so fucking evil.

After a few moments, his laughter died, and he wiped a tear from his eye. A fucking tear.

"You are a breath of fresh air, little treasure." He sighed contentedly.

I frowned with disdain. I didn't think it was funny. Not one little bit. "I'm not fucking you, Ansin. It wasn't part of our deal."

"It was implied, but not to worry; I'll find a way to make it officially part of our arrangement. I always get what I want."

I bet he did. "There's a first time for everything."

"And everything has a price."

We were doing the quotes again, were we? "What separates man from animals is his ability to dream."

He chuckled. "I think you and I are going to be very happy together."

"Over my dead body."

"That can be arranged, little treasure, but let us not go there. Threats are not my style. If I want you dead, it'll just happen."

I felt the heaviness of his words like a punch to the throat. Once again, I believed him. I had to stop letting my guard down and my curiosity get to me. *Trust no one.*

CHAPTER FIFTEEN

The moment we left the airport, dark gray clouds rolled in, and it started to rain. Just like Ansin had said.

Too bad because I wasn't able to see much of the London area as we drove through and headed north. I'd never been to England, and at the rate things were going, I doubted I ever would again.

I'll be lucky to survive another week. Like Dad always said, if you surrounded yourself with bad people, bad things happened.

Speaking of bad, Ansin remained in a meditative state the entire drive, which only amped up my nerves. What did he think would happen? It had to be bad if he needed to center himself for an eight-and-half-hour flight plus another few hours during the drive.

Be optimistic. Maybe he's catching up on sleep?

Just as the sun set, the driver turned down a long dirt road filled with potholes and puddles, finally stopping at an iron gate wedged between twenty-foot-high stone walls.

I was relieved to be here, but nothing about this entrance gave me a good feeling. *Reminds me of Ansin: fuck off!*

Ansin started getting out of the car.

"We're walking from here?" I asked.

"It's for his safety." Ansin gestured to the driver, who didn't move an inch, almost like he wasn't even listening.

"But it's safe enough for me?"

"Not if you're alone. But you have me." He almost smiled, but it fizzled mid-lip.

Crap. Even Ansin couldn't pretend this was entirely safe.

He got out, and with a grimace, I grabbed my purse and followed. The man drove off. Once again, no money was exchanged.

I shook my head. Ansin's mind-control powers thoroughly baffled me. *I hope he doesn't use them on me.* Would I even know if he did? The thought disturbed me.

Ansin pushed on the gate, which opened with a creak. A cold gust of wind kicked up, and my body filled with waves of pinpricks, a sure sign this was a bad place with bad things inside.

"You look cold. Take this." Ansin handed me his black leather jacket.

The temperature wasn't the problem, but I took it anyway. I only had on my jeans and T-shirt that I'd thrown on before heading out to meet Ansin at the café. From there, we took off. No phone charger, toothbrush, or clean undies. I was unprepared for this trip in more ways than one.

"Thanks." I slid on the jacket and watched Ansin sail through the gate. Meanwhile, my feet were having an argument with my brain, which was pretty damned sure it wanted nothing to do with being on Sage's property.

"I told you I would keep you safe, Jeni, but I can't do it if you stay out there."

"I'm not feeling so good. Maybe that sandwich." *Or it's the tiny Seer inside me, yelling not to go in.*

"Do what you need to but make it quick." He marched off, his heavy footsteps crunching over gravel.

He was leaving me here? I looked over my shoulder at the darkness surrounding me. We were in the middle of nowhere.

"Don't forget why you came all this way, little treasure! Your King awaits," Ansin called out.

Right. King was inside, being tortured in the most gruesome of ways. If there was ever a time to step up and be brave, it was now.

Hugging my purse to my chest, I held my breath and stepped through the gate. *Phew!* I half expected to fall into a pit of body organs.

"Hold up. I'm coming." I hurried after Ansin, following the sound of his footsteps. Thank God he was a big guy who made lots of noise when he walked, because I could hardly see where I was going. The rain had stopped, but the sky was overcast and as close to pitch black as it could get.

Ansin didn't slow his pace.

"Hey! Wait for me," I barked, but he didn't stop until he reached what I guessed was the damned castle. I couldn't see squat—just a dark structure with a few shadows and angles that appeared to be several stories tall.

I expected Ansin to ring the doorbell or knock, but instead he waltzed right in.

What the hell? On the other hand, I was beginning to expect this kind of behavior from him. He walked around like he owned the world and answered to no one. Maybe it was true.

I slowly leaned inside the foyer, praying I didn't find people strung up on walls or children and puppies in decorative cages.

But no. The foyer was a small art gallery with beautiful paintings of flowered meadows, horses, and grazing sheep. Modern lighting, mounted to the ten-foot ceiling, illuminated each piece of art, giving the space a relaxing, reflective vibe.

Yeah, don't trust it. Especially because a set of solid wooden doors blocked the view on the other side. What was in there? *Besides the bedroom where they're harvesting King's organs.* For what? Who knew?

Did it really matter?

Like Ariadna said, I needed to believe in my gut. Unfortunately, my gut said, "Run away! Run away!"

Fuck it. I pushed on the doors and spoke into the crack. "Ansin?"

No one replied.

Cautiously, I stepped into the room, which was what I imagined a castle should look like—tall domed ceilings and stained-glass windows on each side of the room. In the center were two red velvet sofas and a chocolate brown armchair. Off in the corner, by a large fireplace, was a grand piano with an unlit candelabra overhead.

The room was huge, but comfy. Elegant and immaculate, too. Not the home of a psycho killer with a fetish for mason jars and kidneys.

I tiptoed through the room, keeping my eyes and ears open for any sign of life. Where was Ansin? Where was that bedroom I'd seen in my visions?

Almost to the next doorway, Ansin and a tall brunette strolled in, both holding snifters of something golden, whisky or brandy. The woman wore a green silk gown and had the longest and shiniest hair I'd ever seen.

"Ah, here she is." Ansin extended his hand in my direction. "Sage, allow me to present Miss Jeni Arnold. Miss Arnold, this is Sage Wellesley."

Ansin seemed awfully friendly with this Sage monster. Was I being set up?

"How do you two know each other?" I asked Ansin, trying not to sound shaken up. "Did you meet in Ten Club?"

"Sage and I go way, *waaay* back." Ansin swiped

his free hand dismissively through the air.

Sage batted her thick black eyelashes at him. "Yes, we do," she sang out. "So many wonderful memories, too." She shifted her gaze to the domed ceiling and smiled as if reliving some great memory.

"Well, unfortunately," Ansin said, "this visit won't be as extensive as my prior ones, Sage. I'm on a tight schedule with my next project."

"Project?" Sage clapped one hand on her glass. "Do tell, Ansin. You know how I love all your debauchery and ventures."

"I would," he said in an overtly charming voice, "but it would ruin the surprise. I know how you love surprises."

"Oh." She chuckled sadistically. "I do."

"Good. Because this one is," he pushed his fingertips together, kissed the tips, and motioned toward the sky, "delicious! It's also why I'm here. I have something you've been craving. Something exotic and rare. Something that will not disappoint, and I'd like to make a trade."

Her dark eyes widened into joyful orbs.

Shit. My blood pressure hit the ancient stone floor. I was the only "thing" he'd brought with him. Ansin was about to betray me.

He continued right on cue, "I would like to trade Jeni here for what you have behind door number one. And, yes, I'm referring to King. I know he's in your bedroom, Sage, so don't pretend otherwise."

My knees began to shake. My heart knocked inside my chest. I needed to get the hell out of here, but I had no clue where I was.

Does it matter? Ansin is about to give you to Princess Chop-Chop.

"Ansin, you fucking asshole," I seethed out my words.

He gave me a stern look and wrapped his hand around my wrist, dropping his drink. Glass shattered on the floor.

"Ow! Let go!" I struggled, trying to pull away, but his grip was a vise.

"If you run, Seer," he snarled, "it'll only make things worse. Sage gets excited by a good chase. Makes her especially violent."

"True." Sage gloated with a smile that melted away. "But, Ansin, why would I trade King for her?"

"Sage, Sage, Sage." Ansin shook his head of black locks. "I'm hurt. Have I ever steered you wrong? This is the only living Seer, and she's powerful. Imagine what you could do with her heart and ovaries. All I want is to kill King. It's a fair trade."

Jesus. This was why Ansin didn't want to tell me his plan. He wanted to trade me for King—the man he wanted to kill. And what better way to do it than grab King while he was incapacitated.

"A Seer, huh?" Sage sized me up, her sinister gaze scanning my body. "What can she do?"

"Fucking let me go!" I protested.

Ansin held onto me tighter, and Sage ignored me. I was nothing more than a squeaking mouse.

"She's still green, but look at her," Ansin urged. "You can taste the power wafting from her organs. Even at this early stage in her development, she's already more gifted than any Seer I've ever met. Imagine what she'll be like if you allow her to ripen ten or twenty years."

My terror now matched my hate for Ansin. I'd rather die, here and now, than "ripen" with Sage for a decade or two.

Sage pushed an index finger to the corner of her mouth. "I don't know… Seers are so erratic. My guest upstairs lost everything because he underestimated them."

"King didn't know how to control them." Ansin waved another dismissive hand. "King's a fool—bit off more than he could chew. But Jeni'll be easy-peasy for you, Sage."

Sage wiggled her lips side to side, deep in thought. "What if I trade something else?"

"Has to be King. He and I have business to settle, and if I know you, you've had your fun and filled your jars. You don't *really* need him anymore."

"One can never have too many hearts of a king, Ansin."

I was going to throw up. For real this time.

"Sage, I would consider it a personal favor if you would make this trade. I'll even throw in Victor's bracelet." Ansin held out the cuff he'd taken off

Victor's body. "This is the real deal. Keeps a person from aging. Can bring them back to life. You can melt it down and make your famous ink with it."

Ink? For what?

Sage's eyes fixated on the bracelet. "Where'd you get that?"

He shrugged. "Victor suffered a misfortune. I happened to be there." He wobbled his hand, making the cuff shimmer under the lights. "It's a good trade."

I raised my hand. "Sorry to throw a wrench in things, but I'm not up for being traded."

"Shut up, Seer," Ansin snarled. "You belong to me now and will do as you are told."

"What the hell is that on her wrist?" Sage pointed a boney finger at my right arm.

I wasn't sure what she meant until I looked at my wrist. I'd completely forgotten about it. King, in all his audacious glory, had decided to tattoo his mark on my wrist—the letter *K*, written in script.

I dropped my wrist and glared at Ansin. *Oops. Fuck you.*

He looked at Sage. "That doesn't mean anything. Ten Club is over."

"Is it? Because King is alive upstairs in a nice new body." She folded her arms over her chest.

"Not for long. I plan to kill him," Ansin replied confidently. I wondered if he really understood how difficult it was to kill King.

"Sorry," she said, "but until he's actually dead,

the rules still apply. Including for this trade right now. Which means no deal. Now, if you wish to trade for something else? Say…a night with you?" She flashed a sadistic smile.

"No thanks. I like my heart exactly where it is," he replied and then looked at me. For a tiny moment I swore I saw a flicker of regret in his eyes. So he was disappointed that he didn't get to double-cross me?

Oh, boo-hoo… Fuck this guy. He made a deal with me and broke it.

"I want to make a trade," I said.

"You?" Sage laughed. "What could you possibly have to trade, Seer? The only thing of value you own is your body, and King still has rights to that."

"My thoughts are fair game. I'll trade you King for one session with me. Ask anything you want. Treasures you've been looking for? People you've been hunting? Maybe you—"

"I want to see my death," Sage threw out.

"Your death?" I asked.

"Yes. I want to know when, where, and how I die," she said.

"Okay. Done." I stretched out my hand to shake on it.

Ansin stepped between us, facing Sage. "Uh-uh. Not so fast. Jeni doesn't know the rules, Sage, but I do. Only agreements made between club members mean anything. But I like this deal, so I'll sponsor it. King in exchange for one session with Jeni, who will tell you everything you want to know about your death."

"Hold on," I said to Ansin. "You want to kill King. I want to save him."

"Why?" Sage asked me.

"Because…" I swallowed my words.

"She loves him," Ansin threw out. "Which means she's not as smart as she looks."

Asshole. I shot a scathing look his way, even though he was probably right. There was no reason on God's messed-up green earth to rationalize my feelings for the man. Still, my feelings weren't theirs to judge.

"He saved my dad," I said. "And to me, that means something." True.

"Well, maybe you and I can work something out later." Ansin winked. He fucking winked. Did he think this was a game?

Hold on. I had to take a moment and roll this situation through my head, because I suddenly wasn't sure if Ansin was playing me or playing Sage.

My mind scrambled through the facts, what I knew and what I didn't. Ansin had showed up at the resort the other night and made an offer: Me in exchange for King's life.

So if he only wanted to kill King and had a way to do it, he would have done it. Period.

Instead, Ansin decided to use his unsubstantiated threat as leverage, knowing I loved King.

How exactly did he know?

I could only guess he'd been watching me for a while. Which meant he'd been watching King, too. How else would Ansin have been there the other night when King and I went to Victor's yacht? Ansin had been following us, waiting to make his move. On me.

The point was, why go through all that simply to fly here to the UK and trade me away for King? Ansin had been given multiple opportunities to get to King before this.

He was playing Sage. *And yet, I magically don't blame myself for jumping to the worst possible conclusion about him.* In fact, he'd used it to his advantage. Having me appear confused, angry, and authentically terrified sold his little scheme to Sage, hadn't it?

"Yes. Fine," I said to Ansin with a bitter tinge in my tone, "we can work out something later. But I want your protection from people like her." I jerked my head in Sage's direction.

His gold-and-black eyes softened for a fraction of a second. It was only meant for me to see. "Always."

I felt the sincerity of his words spike through me, and like the cold wind outside, it reached my bones and the backs of my knees.

"I don't give a crap what you two do with King," said Sage. "I was done with him anyway. Bastard keeps calling out for his wife." Sage shook her head. "Love disgusts me."

Why am I not surprised?

Ansin and Sage shook hands.

"Shall we go to the dining hall?" Sage gestured toward a set of wooden double doors to the side of this room.

I looked at Ansin. Not for permission, but because I didn't know this bitch, and she was creepy as fuck.

He jerked his head. "Let's get this over with."

CHAPTER SIXTEEN

I set my purse on the couch and followed Sage into her dining hall. It was quite the room with vaulted ceilings, torch sconces, and a mahogany table, long enough to seat twenty people, stretching the length of the cavernous space. Overhead, chandeliers made from the skulls of tiny animals hung in tribute to Sage's cruel nature.

And someone gets the prize for world's worst decorator.

"Take a seat." Sage pointed to a chair opposite her at the center of the table.

I pulled out the chair, noting the strange carving on the back. A human heart. This woman was nuts.

Ansin sat at the head of the table, away from us.

"Come closer, Ansin, I don't bite. Much," Sage said.

He held up his palms. "Don't want to interfere with the session. This Seer hates my fucking guts. I'd only be a distraction."

I didn't hate his guts. I just didn't trust him.

"All right." I inhaled slowly. "First I need to

relax. So if we could all be silent for a moment, it'll help speed things along."

"I thought you were supposed to be powerful?" she pushed.

"I said she was green, Sage. Give the girl a minute. I promise you won't be disappointed." Ansin folded his meaty, scarred-up arms across his broad chest and leaned back in his chair.

Knowing King's life was on the line, I closed my eyes and tilted back my head. *Focus. Focus.* I'd never tried using my gift under this kind of pressure. *Come on, Jeni. Come on. You can do this…*

Fuck! I was getting nothing but a white room with white walls again. I had to be prepared to make something up—something believable just in case. *You can do this. Just relax. Push your mind. See, Jeni. See Sage dying. It's something you might actually enjoy watching. See…*

Suddenly, I was flying through that same dark sky again. The night was foggy below, allowing me a view of the patches of lights on the ground, same as before. Above me, the stars twinkled over a moonless night. And like the last time, my body started falling to the ground, through clouds and pockets of cold air, through that stone roof.

I blinked, realizing I was here in this very room, sitting in this very chair. *What the hell?* Ansin stood behind Sage, his knife drawn and ready to slice her throat from ear to ear, just like he'd done to Victor.

My eyes flew open, and I locked eyes with Sage.

"I'm so sorry," I said.

"You can't see my death?" Her eyes lit up, and she cackled, smacking her pale hand on the table. "I knew it! I knew I'd never die. Yes!"

"No," I said, "I'm sorry because you die here in this room. Tonight." I grinned just as Ansin's arm reached across her neck and sliced deep.

Sage's hands flew to the wound, her eyes wide with terror as her blood gushed onto the table.

I looked away, covering my mouth. I couldn't say I felt sorry for her, not after everything she'd done to King, but I didn't get off on it either. The only consolation was there'd be one less Ten Club member killing people's moms, dads, brothers, sisters, and children.

With a final, gruesome gurgle, Sage's body slumped forward, and her blood crept across the table. I scooted back in my chair, not wanting to come in contact with it.

"You all right?" Ansin asked as I quietly stared at Sage, swallowing my horror.

I shook my head no, but said, "I think so."

"Good. Now you need to look away," he said.

"Why-why?"

He reached down and cut away the top of her dress. Her collarbone—what I could see of it—was covered in an elaborate tribal tattoo, almost like a necklace.

"What's that?" I asked.

"A ward of sorts. Keeps her from dying. Keeps

her from aging."

Like the ring King gave my dad. "I had no idea that kind of thing could be permanently tattooed on."

"Not many people have these because not many people know how to do them. Sage was one." He raised his hand with the knife.

"What are you doing?" I gasped.

"Unless you want her coming back to life and hunting you down, I have to remove her head. Which is why I said that *you* need to look away."

I'm going to be sick. "I think I'll go find King." I stood from my chair.

"Not without me. Sage has quite the arsenal, and every square inch of this castle has wards and traps to keep out thieves."

"Oh. Lovely."

He stared and raised an expectant brow.

"Sorry. Looking away," I said.

I turned my body and stared at the stone wall, trying to block out the sounds of flesh being cut and bones being broken. I didn't know what kind of person it took to perform such a fucked-up act, but apparently Ansin was one of them.

He's definitely more twisted than King. I made a mental note to never cross him. At the same time, I couldn't ignore Ansin had to do it to protect me.

"All right. Done. Let's go look for King. And, Jeni, I strongly advise you don't look this way."

I was already turning to leave the room. Of

course, when someone tells you not to look, what's the first thing you do?

Oh crap. I looked. Exposed neckbones, bloody tendons, and everything gory one would expect to see when a person was relieved of their head.

The sandwich in my stomach launched up and out, splattering on the stone floor.

"Jeni, I fucking told you…"

Ansin's voice faded into nothing as the room started spinning. Right before it turned black.

CHAPTER SEVENTEEN
ANSIN

"Jeni, Jeni, Jeni." I shook my head at the Seer, who lay passed out on the dining room floor, a mere four feet from Sage's headless body. Blood everywhere.

I hate this kind of crap.

People who knew me—not many—always asked why I wore cheap T-shirts and leather pants. This was why.

I went to the kitchen, which was just off the dining room, and grabbed some towels near the big metal sink.

"Hate cleaning blood," I griped.

I wiped the sticky red liquid from my pants and then removed my shirt, tossing it into the sink. I washed my hands, arms and face, too. God only knew what sort of poisons Sage had in her blood. She was always experimenting and creating potions with her collection of pickled body parts. She claimed they gave her powers. I thought she was just a fucking psycho. The only thing she was good at was mixing her dream drugs and tattoo inks. I'd be sure to steal her recipes before I left.

Now shirtless and clean, I went to Sage's fridge and helped myself to a beer. I knew the only things safe to drink in this castle were her top-shelf scotch, which she kept locked in a cupboard, and this. Everything else was for her "guests," which was how she probably got King into her bed.

Likely micro-dosed him over the course of a few hours. That was usually how she did it. Give her enemy the tiniest amount of her dream drug. They didn't even notice. All of a sudden, their guard was down, and they felt right at home. Sage offered them another drink. *Sure, what the hell,* they'd say. *If she were going to poison me, she would have done it by now.* The unsuspecting guest got another dose. Then a third and a fourth. Before they knew what was happening, they were in a dream world, completely entranced by whatever Sage wanted them to see. Meanwhile, Sage was carving out their organs.

I had to hand it to her, the technique worked nicely because her victims never put up a fight. But I had to wonder what she gave King to drink. He knew her tricks. *Hell, the bastard probably taught her some of them.*

I polished off my beer and returned to Jeni in the other room. She was a beauty. Her long wavy brown hair, her inquisitive brown eyes, and her sexy little lips. No, she wasn't the kind of woman men tripped over in the streets. She was the kind of pretty only men of substance noticed, the quiet muse in the dark corner of a café, her nose buried in a book. (History was her thing. I'd done my research.) She was also the sort of woman who stood by the people she cared for. She understood that family and loyalty were everything.

How did I know all this?

Like I said, I'd done my research. For example, I knew she'd bartered with King so her father would be healed. And I knew she was going to hurt when I finally killed King. Which I would do when the time was right.

I'd been preparing to take him out ever since I'd heard of his sudden return.

Twenty-five years he'd been gone. Twenty-five.

For the first few years, most club members believed he was preoccupied with something. Perhaps a woman? Perhaps a new addition to his arsenal. But when no one came to collect our Ten Club dues, we knew something had happened to him. Members were getting arrested for their crimes. Judges and politicians stopped protecting us. Word started getting out about Ten Club.

After that, things turned into the Wild West until Serina, a longtime club member with ambition, called in enough favors to be voted in as the new "King."

I hated that bitch. She was always too greedy, wanting a slice of everyone's pie. At least King left us alone. We paid our dues. We called when we needed something we couldn't handle. We showed up to a meeting once every few decades. If anyone broke rules—like stealing from club members or welching on deals—then one of King's Seers would show up and issue a warning.

That was all it took.

Because everyone knew the next visit would be from King if you fucked up again. And no one wanted to end up with their head in a jar in his infamous warehouse. For the record, those heads never died.

So when Serina took over, trying to insert herself in our business, no one was happy. We paid ten fucking billion dollars a year each to belong to Ten Club, and the entire premise was that membership bought us immunity for any crimes. It bought our freedom to pursue whatever we liked. Nowhere did anyone sign up for a bullshit share-my-evil-loot model. Serina wanted to know what people had in their arsenals, what they were trying to acquire, and she wanted dibs.

After a few decades of that, some of us began contemplating overthrowing Serina, but I questioned what I was really getting out of Ten Club. I didn't need access to corrupt lawyers and judges. I didn't need deal enforcement with other members. I was powerful enough to handle all that on my own.

What I really wanted was to get rid of anyone more powerful than me, who might try to acquire my family members after I restarted my bloodline.

To Ten Club members, we would be mere objects to collect, like the Seers.

Ten Club had to go.

Then King returned. A gift. He did most of the dirty work for me, and now all I had left to do was eliminate him. So, yes. I was absolutely going to kill King, because King was still going to come after me.

And now I've kept my word to Jeni. Our new deal stipulated I come here and save him. Which I'd done. *I never promised I wouldn't kill him afterward.* The only trick was keeping Jeni in my corner. It would serve me better in the long run. She needed to witness King attempting to eliminate me first. I would defend myself.

I scooped Jeni from the floor, her arms flopping to her sides as I carried her to the living room.

I deposited her on the sofa, where she let out a groan. "King…" she muttered.

"Not King. Ansin," I said.

Her eyes fluttered open. "What happened?"

"You looked is what happened."

"Oh…"

"I'd offer you water, but I doubt any of it is safe to drink in this house. How about a beer?"

"No. No beer." She pointed to her purse near her feet. "I have juice."

I grabbed it, and she took a small sip.

"Better?"

"I think so." She sat up, pressing her palms to her eyes. "I need to go find King now."

"I'll go. You stay here and res—"

"No."

I smiled. "Don't trust me, little treasure?"

"What do you think?"

"I hope you're not holding a little decapitation against me?"

She stared blankly.

"I had no choice," I said, attempting to hide my amusement. "Sage would have woken up tomorrow with you on her hit list, and I couldn't have that, now could I?" True.

Jeni slowly swung her feet to the floor, swiping her long hair from her face. "I'm fine. I'll go with you to find him."

So she didn't trust me. Good for her.

I helped her to her feet. "I know where he is, but you must walk behind me. Like I said, Sage loved her traps, and this house is filled with them."

"How will you know where they are?"

"I helped her install some—a trade for some of her dream juice."

"Dream juice?" She raised a brow.

"It was her specialty. It's basically liquid hypnosis—can make a person believe they're somewhere they're not."

Jeni crinkled her nose. "Did she give that stuff to King?"

"Probably."

I noted a sadness in her eyes.

"What is it?" Not that I felt sympathy for her,

but my curiosity was piqued.

"Nothing. Let's get him out of that room. And then I want to burn this place to the ground."

"Excellent suggestion." No one should be allowed in here after we left. It was far too dangerous. Not that I cared about any person stupid enough to wander in, but we didn't need someone getting a hold of Sage's arsenal. After I picked through the good stuff, of course.

"Let's go rescue your King." I turned and headed toward the arched doorway that led to Sage's private study, her expensive Scotch stash, and to the staircase that led upstairs.

"Stay close. Only step on the black squares with crosses."

"Okay. I'm not even going to ask."

CHAPTER EIGHTEEN
JENI

So the rest of Sage's castle was a house of horror. Dark, smelly, and dusty. Nothing like the downstairs area, which I assumed she used to impress or disarm people when they entered the home.

Upstairs, which was lit with more torch sconces, Sage had brown-and-black checkered runners on the stone floors. The black squares had brown crosses and the brown squares had black. The point was, the difference was subtle, but according to Ansin, one wrong step could land you with a spear in your leg.

"You really helped her booby-trap this place?" I asked, following Ansin down the narrow corridor.

"It's common for club members to barter for goods and services. I am particularly good at medieval warfare."

Really? "How did that happen?"

"I spent time with Richard I, running his private security, more or less. He had a lot of enemies. He loved war."

To think that Ansin was there during the 1100s was pretty amazing. "So you actually knew Richard the Lionheart?"

"Yes."

"Who else did you mingle with? I mean, of historical significance?"

"The list is far too long, but to be honest, the more interesting people—the ones who left a memorable mark—were never the ones you read about in those books you love."

"How do you know which books I like?" Oh, that was right. He'd been watching me.

"I always do my research on people, whether it's to kill them or—"

"Blackmail them into being your wife?"

He was silent for a long moment as we continued our careful steps down the long hallway.

"For the record, you're the first," he threw out.

"Am I supposed to feel special now?"

"Yes."

Yeah, I bet he thought that. "I'm not sure I agre—"

"Stop," he barked.

"Excuse me? Don't tell me to shut u—"

"Stop. Don't move." Ansin froze in front of me.

Oh no. "What's wrong?"

"You smell that?" he asked.

Yep. I sure did. The air smelled like farts with a hint of death.

"I smell sage."

Fuck. "Is she back?" I looked over my shoulder, wondering if that crazy bitch had somehow managed to put her head back on and was now coming for us.

"No, the herb. Sage. It was her favorite. She mixed it into all her dream products."

"I have no idea what that means."

Ansin hung his head. "Son of a bitch."

My heart raced. My legs burned with the urge to run. "What? What's wrong?"

Ansin turned carefully and faced me. "She had a gas."

I crinkled my nose. *Explains the smell.* "I hope she's in a better place now?"

"No, Jeni. She made her dream drug into a gas. She'd been working on it forever. I never thought she'd figure it out, but she did."

"I'm not following."

"We triggered one of her traps. We've just been drugged."

"You mean with that dream stuff? What do we do?"

"Her bedroom is at the end of this hall. That's where she has King. But we won't make it. We have about ten seconds before the dreams kick in."

Oh God. "What kind of dreams?"

"Without someone to direct you, you'll either dream of your worst nightmare or, if you're lucky, something you desire."

My worst nightmare. So I had a fifty-fifty chance

of dreaming I was here in this castle? I didn't like the sound of that at all. Nor did I like the idea of dreaming of King—the only thing I desired.

"We can't stay in this hallway." Ansin took my hand. "We need to go in there. I'm sorry." He pointed to a door about ten feet away.

"Sorry? Why sorry?"

He tugged me along, ignoring my question. "Careful. Watch your step." He pushed on the door and yanked me inside.

The smell. Oh God, the smell. I covered my face and retched. "What is *that?*"

"Sage's storeroom and laboratory, for lack of a better term. I won't turn on the lights because it'll only fuck with your head—the last thing you need right now. One second to go…"

I felt my body relaxing against my will. Loose neck, loose knees, a warm sensation in my chest. "It's starting."

"I know." Ansin tugged on my hand as he sank to the floor. "Put your back against the door."

I drifted down, sitting next to him, gripping his hand like it was a lifeline to keep me safe.

"What's going to happen, Ansin?" I mumbled.

"I'm going to tell you what to dream about. And when you wake tomorrow, it'll feel like it was all real, but it's not. You just have to remember none of it was real."

My mind began to puddle, thoughts losing their firmness, drifting away like wisps of steam I couldn't catch.

"Jeni," I heard Ansin's deep, dark voice echoing in the background of my mind, "you're going to dream of a beautiful house near the ocean. The walls that surround it are high. The air is fresh. You are safe and happy. You spend your days reading all the books you love. You spend your nights with me in bed. Making love. Being cherished. You will feel like you're in heav-heaven…"

He wanted me to dream of him? Even in my state of limp-noodle-mindedness, I knew it was a dirty trick. But I would rather dream of him than my worst nightmare. *Or King.*

Ansin's words seeped into me, through my skin, deep into my bones, and infused with my mind.

"I hope you dream of my constant rejection of you," I muttered to Ansin before falling into a deep sleep.

I love it here. I dipped my toes in the warm salty waves while gazing out across miles of crystal-clear blue water. To my sides were endless stretches of powder white sand kissed by fresh clean air.

Crete three thousand years ago. No planes. No cell towers or motors. Just beach. Ocean. And Ansin. I sighed contentedly. *Ansin…*

I'd never felt so good. So fulfilled. Ansin was sleeping now, because he'd spent the night catering to my every whim. He'd read to me—my book of favorite quotes—before feeding me warm soft bread, figs, and savory cheeses.

Wine. The wine. It was the most delicious thing I'd ever tasted. Notes of chocolate, berries, plums, and smoke.

Afterward, he kissed my body head to toe and made love to me. Not fucked. But loved. Every movement had been purposeful and skilled. He worked me over slowly with every thrust, flexing his strong naked body over me.

The strangest part was that his skin wasn't scarred anymore. It was smooth, like cream mixed with caramel. He was perfect. A dream.

After that, I drifted off—limp, glowing, and feeling the sort of happiness a person like me only dreamed of.

Now it was a new day, and my heart raced thinking about the chance to do it all over again tonight when he woke.

Drip, drip, drip.

I looked over my shoulders. What was that sound?

Drip, drip, drip.

There wasn't a cloud in the sky. Where was it coming from?

Drip, drip…

My shoulder felt cold and wet all of a sudden. I got to my feet and ran my hand over the spot. My skin was perfectly dry, and the air around me was warm. A perfect sunny day.

The cold sensation turned to heat. Then hotter, hotter.

"Ow!" I slapped my shoulder, trying to put out the invisible fire.

My eyes flew open. Ansin leaned into me, his back to the door and his body hunched. Above the door were shelves filled with glass jars and…

I jumped to my feet, sending Ansin falling sideways on the floor. *Oh God!* I covered my mouth. *Eyeballs.*

One of the jars had tipped over and—

I turned my head slowly and looked at my shoulder. A white goo covered it. It smelled like alcohol and some other chemical. Probably formaldehyde or something.

"Ew. Yuck!" I turned around, hoping to find something to wipe it off with, immediately regretting my choice. So many body parts in jars. Hands. Feet. Hearts. Squishy red blobs. Livers maybe? All organized—no pun intended—on shelves.

Why? Why? Why? Why would anyone want so many people parts? I closed my eyes tight, wishing I could erase what I'd just seen. Row after row, stretching the length of the room, were jars filled with Sage's gruesome collection. A large window at the end had a desk below it. I assumed that was where Sage had conducted her business.

"Hey, wake up." I gave Ansin a kick. Nothing.

Was he dead? I stared, watching his bare chest

rise and fall in a steady rhythm. His muscled abs were covered in fine lines. More of those scars. I guessed I hadn't noticed last night because I was too messed up in the head after watching Sage die.

Well, at least *we* were still alive.

"Ansin?" He twitched but didn't wake. At least he'd avoided being covered in eyeball goo. This place was horrible. Reminded me of King's warehouse.

King! I forgot about King. I had to go find him, but I still felt woozy. What had been in that dream stuff?

I scrubbed my face with my hands. I needed air, but that window seemed so far away, and I'd have to walk past all those jars.

No choice, Jeni. I wasn't about to go into that hallway without a clear head.

I stared down at the stone floor, refusing to look at the towering shelves to my sides. The odor was beyond putrid.

I got to the desk and leaned over it, careful not to touch any of the items on top—notebooks, a mortar and pestle, small glass test tubes. I popped the latch at the center of the panes, and both sides of the window swung in.

A gust of cold fresh air poured into the room and filled my lungs with the scent of the green grass outside. Off in the distance, horses grazed next to a small stream. It was just like the paintings in the foyer entrance.

My head began to clear immediately, and I went back to check on Ansin. Maybe the fresh air was helping him, too.

"Ansin? Hey, wake up." I gave him another nudge with my foot, but he was still out cold, in dreamland.

Strange. A part of me felt a sense of loss when I looked at him now. I'd been so happy in that dream. And the sex felt real. Every detail—the way he moved, the texture of his soft skin, the way his back flexed beneath my fingertips when he drove his thick cock into me. It had been just as real as any memory.

My breasts and groin began to heat recalling the touch of his rough hands. *But it wasn't real. It wasn't real,* I told myself. Ansin had been right. He said I would wake up feeling otherwise.

Why had he done that to me? He planted that dream.

I hope you enjoyed your dream of me telling you no. Hope you wake up with blue balls.

"Ansin?" I tried one more time to wake him. Nada. I should wait for him, but I worried about King. Was he all right? Was he still alive? Somewhere in between?

I scooted Ansin's muscled limp frame out of the way and carefully stepped out into the hall. I sniffed the air, which still held a putrid aroma, but there was no hint of sage. A good sign.

I focused my attention on the length of the hall.

At the very end was another large window. Ansin said that Sage's bedroom was down that way. I only hoped I didn't encounter more of her traps.

Tiptoeing, I navigated my way to the large window and opened it. To my left was a red door. On the other side had to be King, but what else would I find in there?

Probably more of that dream crap.

I sucked in a big breath of fresh air and opened the door. The bed from my vision sat in the middle of the room, but the red velvety curtains were drawn around it. I couldn't see if King was inside or what shape he'd be in. I'd have to go in and be fast.

I spotted another window just opposite the door. I rushed over and pulled open the panes, allowing more sweet air to fill the room. I exhaled and breathed it in, noting a foul stench nearby. Death.

I hoped it wasn't King. But how could it be? He couldn't die. Not yet. My eyes swept the room, immediately finding the source of the odor. On the nightstand were more jars.

My heart sank. I'd seen them in my vision, too. I knew what they were.

Poor King. No one deserved that kind of torture. He'd been cut open, had his organs removed, and then left to heal or regenerate or whatever he did when his body came back, good as new. All just so Sage could repeat the process.

Sick.

I walked over to the bed, placed my hands on the seams of the curtains, and closed my eyes. Whatever was in this bed might be worse than anything I'd seen so far. Was I ready?

Probably not.

With a swoosh, I parted the curtains. King lay there with a thick satin blanket covering his torso, his arms to his sides. He looked as beautiful as ever, his lips relaxed, that regal set of straight black brows arched perfectly across his forehead. Thick silky lashes fanned out over his cheekbones, and a wash of inky stubble covered his square jaw. He looked like a sleeping Greek god, too beautiful for words. He was back. Alive again. Shiny new body.

I sighed with relief. "King? Can you hear me?" I sat on the edge of the bed and touched his arm. "King? You're safe now. Sage is gone."

"Mmmm…" he groaned.

"Open your eyes. Tell me you're okay."

Suddenly, his arm reached out and pulled me down. He rolled on top of me, pinning my hands above my head.

"What are you doing?" I gasped.

The blankets were tangled between our bodies, but I could feel he was hard.

King buried his head in the crook of my neck and began kissing the tender skin. "You feel so good. I missed you."

I winced, knowing those words weren't for me. How could they be? His mind was probably off somewhere with Mia.

Still, my body instantly heated. Maybe it was because I'd just spent the night dream-fucking Ansin and my body needed a real release. Maybe it was because my body remembered King. It remembered how good he'd made me feel. Or maybe it was the baby hormones. Either way, I couldn't help enjoying the sensation of his weight on top of me, even if I knew his arousal wasn't for me.

"King, King, wake up," I whispered. "It's me, Jeni."

He kept kissing my neck, grinding against me.

"King, you have to—" I noticed my back felt wet and warm all of a sudden. *What the hell is that? What the hell!* Sage had been repeatedly dissecting King in this bed and—

It was his blood! The bed was soaked with it.

"Ah! No! No!" I pushed King off me and hopped from the bed. He tumbled through the curtains on the other side, falling to the floor.

I pulled off my shirt and threw the thing to the floor. It had a big red splotch on the back. "This place is horrible!" I kicked it away. "Horrible!"

The sound of King's moan filled the room.

I rushed around the bed to find him naked and on his side. He had blood on his back but no cuts or open wounds. He did, however, have some new body art. Around his collarbone was the same tattoo I'd seen on Sage. Black with an intricate woven pattern.

I kneeled next to him. "Are you okay? Can you hear me?"

"Why did you throw me on the floor?" His pale gray eyes fluttered open.

"I'm sorry. You were dreaming and…" I didn't want to say the rest. It didn't matter.

"What are you doing here, Seer?" he asked.

"My name is still Jeni. And I'm here because you're here. I saw that crazy bitch cutting you open in one of my visions."

King sat up slowly. "And you thought to rescue me. Are you mad, woman? Where is Sage now?"

I hated that he didn't care I'd come to help him. Not a thank-you to be found. "Um. You're welcome. And Sage and her head are both downstairs in the dining room. But don't worry, Ansin made sure they're not talking to each other anymore."

"Who?" King rubbed his forehead, looking groggy.

I tried not to look at his naked body, still partially aroused, even if it was the one thing I couldn't forget and longed for. He was all lean, hard muscles with beautiful olive skin. His cock was long and thick, and he knew how to use it.

"Ansin, the Ten Club member," I said.

"He's here?"

"Yes. I—"

"Where is Ansin now?" King got to his feet and walked over to an old vanity in the corner where a pile of clothes sat neatly folded on top. I assumed they were his clothes because he slid on the black pants. "Sonofabitch. Fucking Sage." King caught a glimpse of his bare chest in the mirror and stroked the circular tattoo.

"Sage seemed very excited about harvesting your heart multiple times." *So gross.* "She probably didn't know you can't die."

"No. She didn't," he grumbled, pissed off as ever. "And now I have one more obstacle between me and death. These fucking things are impossible to remove." King slid on his white shirt and began buttoning, starting at the top. He didn't seem to care about the blood covering his back. I seriously wondered why Sage had played "dice up the king" in her own bed. Had she planned to sleep in it after? *Nasty.*

"So where is Ansin?" King asked.

"Asleep in Sage's body part mart."

"Passed out from one of her dream potions?" He pushed his feet into his black dress shoes, not bothering with his socks.

"Yes, but I need to talk to you."

"After I kill him." King turned and marched toward the door.

I rushed to block him. "No. I brought him here to save you."

"What? You went to that evil fuck and made a deal? What did he want in exchange?"

"That's not important."

"You're correct. It is not. Because I am going to

kill him all the same." King moved to sidestep me, but I blocked him again.

"The Seers have been playing us, King. They don't plan to release your soul. They are not going to let you cross over to be with Mia. They are planning something completely different."

"What are you talking about?" His thick brows knitted together.

I put my hand over my stomach. "I'm pregnant. It's yours."

He stared coldly. "You are…pregnant."

I nodded.

"If this is some ploy to—"

"No. It's not. I'm carrying Ariadna. I saw it in a vision. I was holding her as a baby. But it's her. I recognized her eyes and mouth—just like yours."

"How's that possible, Jeni? Seers cannot come back that way. Reincarnation has never happened."

"How the hell should I know?" And how could he be so sure? He wasn't a Seer, and they weren't the most open people. "Maybe it has something to do with you being the father, and well, I am a Seer, like her first mother. Maybe that somehow enabled it to happen?"

"Ask them."

"They won't tell me anything, King. They keep saying I'm supposed to play my part and earn my stripes by figuring everything out on my own. Now I have, and I don't like it. I don't trust them."

He placed his hands on his hips. "I can't think

straight. I need fresh air."

King walked back across the room toward the open window and inhaled slowly, and I could see the fog lifting from his face, that vibrant alertness returning to his pale gray eyes.

"Why are you in your bra?" King asked.

"My shirt got dirty." *While you were dry humping me in a pool of your own blood.* I couldn't think of anything worse than that. "Who cares? The bigger question is what are we going to do?"

"About what?"

"Ariadna. Your daughter. She changes everything if she's like her mother. Is she? I mean, will she be?"

"In what way?"

"Time travel? Because I can only think of one reason the Seers would go through all this trouble to bring Ariadna back, and it's not for her to stay here and help you fix things."

King tilted back his head of thick dark hair and groaned.

He got it now. He'd connected the same damned dots I had.

"I'm right, aren't I?" I said. "She can make sure you never meet Mia, that you marry that Hagne woman and take your intended place as Lord of the Seers three thousand years ago."

"Yes." King groaned. "Which means Ariadna can't be born, yet I could never bring myself to harm her. Nor would I allow anyone else to."

Phew. I knew King had his dark side, but for a second there, he'd scared me. "What do we do? Because if that's the Seers' plan, all this goes away someday. You, me, Mia, Arch, and even Ariadna."

He stared at the floor for a long moment, his strong jaw pulsing with tension. "I will have to train her and educate her myself—make sure she does not carry out their wishes. There is no other choice. It would be what Mia would want anyway."

Part of me, a big part, rejoiced. I finally got my wish. King wouldn't leave. Not yet. The other part of me felt, well, as expected. He wouldn't be staying for me. "Are you sure this is what you want? I mean, I could raise her on my own—"

"You cannot train another Seer. You yourself are far too new at this, and Ariadna will be more powerful than you. I will see to her raising. You need not worry."

I felt wounded. "Of course I'm worried. She's mine."

"If what you say is true, then she is *my* daughter. Mine and Mia's. You are merely the baby's vessel."

"Baby? What baby?" A shirtless Ansin appeared in the doorway, his black hair disheveled.

"Who the fuck are you?" King asked.

The energy spiked in the room. Was it King on the defensive? Ansin? Both?

Ansin dipped his head. "I'm the man who's going to kill you, Ansin Bastuli at your service."

"The third and final member." King smiled.

"You're much younger than I remember."

"What can I say? You cleaned up Ten Club, and I went shopping. Found lots of very interesting items in the members' arsenals."

So Ansin used to look older?

Ansin continued, "But my most prize possession has your name on it, King." Ansin patted the knife on his belt. I'd never really taken a good look, but the black handle had an intricate silver circle. I was beginning to think it wasn't an ordinary knife. He'd used it to sneak up on both Victor and Sage. Both were powerful and didn't put up a fight.

King chuckled and shook his head. "You are just as cocky as I remember. I'll be sure to have it noted on your headstone."

A dark shadow zipped across the room, heading straight at Ansin, who ducked. I'd seen that thing kill before. Not one person ever saw it coming. Ansin had.

Ansin unsheathed his knife and charged at King. Ansin flew back, hitting the wall, King's shadow swirled around his head, and Ansin swiped at it with his knife. The shadow moved away, and Ansin got to his feet to take another run at King.

"Wait! No." I stepped between him and King. "Ansin, we had a deal."

"I agreed to save him from Sage," Ansin said, his eyes filled with hate and venom. "I never said I wouldn't kill him after."

"It was implied," I argued, my words coming

out fast, "and you're free to disagree with that, but if you touch him, I won't marry you. I won't have your kids." I wasn't going to anyway, but he didn't know that.

"What's this?" King growled.

"Nothing," I explained. "I had to make a deal with him."

"Only agreements between club members stand," King spat at Ansin. "You know that. And if you'd like to kill me, be my guest, but you'll be very disappointed."

"Ten Club no longer exists," Ansin threw out. "And yes, I'd very much like to take your life. How about now? Is now good for you?"

King said casually, "I am sorry to inform you that it is *your* day to die. Not mine." That shadow took another swipe at Ansin, who ran his knife at it.

"What the hell is that thing?" he said, spinning on his heel, watching it fade into a wall.

I turned to King. "Stop! None of this matters anymore. What Ariadna told you the night of the massacre isn't true. Think about it. She said that the Seers won't release your soul until you completely obliterate Ten Club. But she also said you had to erase your footsteps—three thousand years of them. It's impossible, King. They were never going to let you be free. Their plan was always this. Have you kill Ten Club so it would be safe to bring back Ariadna. So she could grow up and then fulfill her duty. So what's the point now of killing Ansin?"

"He is still a threat to you," King said to me while staring Ansin down. "He only thinks of Seers as objects to be used."

Ansin laughed, still panting with excitement. "Says the man who brought back a few dozen Seers from the dead just so he could force them to do his dirty work." Ansin looked at me. "He slaughtered them the moment they tried to get free."

"They wanted to take over Ten Club," King threw back casually. "I did not feel that would be such a wise idea. As for Jeni, she knows she cannot trust me. I've made no secret of what or who I am. She makes her own choices, and she is free to go at any time."

Ansin shrugged. "And she knows she can't trust me. Yet she still jumped in bed with me. Or will." He winked. "How was that dream, little treasure?"

Were they really discussing this? They were missing the goddamned point!

I threw my hands in the air. "Yes, I'm aware you're both not safe for me. You're both dangerous, double-crossing, power-hungry liars. But this is a new game now. I won't allow my baby to be used by these fucking women. And I don't believe for one minute that having her go back three thousand years to undo everything will help anyone but the Seers. I. Don't. Trust. Them."

"You're pregnant?" Ansin asked, his eyes fixed on my stomach.

"Yes," I snarled. "And if you try to lay a hand

on her—"

"Did you say she'll be able to time travel?" Ansin's expression was pure shock—wide eyes, slack jaw. I'd never seen him with his guard down, and it felt surreal. Ansin was actually having a genuine reaction to something instead of his typical calculated responses. Why?

Only one reason came to mind. "You can't have her, Ansin. I'll kill you myself before I let you get anywhere near her."

"If what you say is true," Ansin spoke with an unusually soft voice, "then she can stop my people from being slaughtered."

"Okay. *What?* I think we just established that Ariadna isn't going anywhere. Or bringing anyone back. Or being used. Or manipulated. Or—"

"Jeni." Ansin stepped closer to me. "I watched my entire family be taken out. My mother and I barely escaped, and she used everything she had left in her to curse me rather than heal herself. She made sure I wouldn't die until I reestablished our people's bloodline. I tried, again and again, to find ways to bring them back, and I failed.

"Then one day, I came across this, Diviciacus' dagger—the druid legends say it was a gift directly from God. I don't know, and I don't care. All I know is it can cut through any spell. It protects whoever carries it from their enemies. I almost used it to end my life, but I couldn't bring myself to do it. Not without doing the one thing I hadn't tried to fulfill my duty to my people. That was finding you—someone powerful enough to carry a child with my bloodline. And while I assume you enjoyed those dreams last night, I'm no fool. You have been calculating a way to get out of our arrangement."

I shrugged. "Maybe."

"Ariadna's gift might be a detriment to you two," he added, "but not for me or my people."

"So what are you saying?" I asked. "That our deal is off if I promise to make Ariadna go back and try to save your family?"

"He cannot ask that." King stepped forward. "I will not allow it, and he already knows you cannot commit Ariadna to anything. Any deal struck must be with her directly."

I flashed a look at King. "I wasn't going to agree. I wanted clarity."

Ansin winked at me. Fucking winked again. "Sorry, Jeni. Our deal stands. It's my insurance policy in case Ariadna is unable or unwilling to help me. But I will say this. She gets my sword."

"You don't have a sword. It's a knife." King's eyes grew colder.

"One that we both know can easily kill you, so watch yourself, King."

Was this true? Could his dagger really cut the cord between King and me and take him out? Ansin had killed Victor and Sage—two very powerful individuals—with ease. Whatever protection or wards they'd had on them had been completely useless. Of course, Ansin had needed to remove Victor's bracelet and Sage's head to stop them from coming back, but he'd definitely killed them. So I had to assume his knife would do the job with King.

I looked at King, who wasn't arguing about its efficacy.

"You will stay away from my daughter," he growled. "And you will stay away from my Seer." King walked up beside me, grabbed my wrist, and showed his mark to Ansin.

Now he was trying to claim ownership? *What the hell?*

Ansin stepped forward. "Ten Club is dead. And Jeni is mine now. The deal was struck. She made it free and clear in order to save your evil ass. She must honor it. You know she has to."

"What's he talking about?" I asked King.

"It's nothing," King said dismissively.

"No. Not nothing," Ansin interjected. "A Seer's promise is her bond. If she breaks it, she will be punished."

"By who?" I asked.

"Didn't your buddy, King here, bother to explain anything to you? The Seers enforce their rules," Ansin said. "You break 'em, you pay. Their entire world is based on the philosophy of balance. If you get, you give. If you do harm, you have to repay with a sacrifice."

I scoffed. "I didn't agree to that."

"You don't have to," King said coldly. "It's

simply the way they do business."

Was this the reason the Seers kept pushing back when I asked for help? I didn't know, and honestly, I didn't give a shit anymore. I was done with them. Their games, their lies, their manipulations. I might have Seer blood, but I wasn't on their team.

Team me. And I would do anything to protect this baby, including aligning myself with the two most dangerous men on the planet. Who else could I turn to if I planned on going up against a clan of Seers? Dead or not, they were still powerful. They'd created a freaking hurricane. They'd ripped King's soul from his body and bound it to me so he couldn't die and cross over. The Seers might not be a part of this physical world, but they sure as hell knew how to manipulate everyone and everything in it.

"So where does this leave us three?" I asked.

"I cannot kill him. Not now." Ansin threaded his fingers through his thick black hair. "King is the only one who can train Ariadna properly."

Okay. I took his words with a grain of salt, but it made sense.

I looked at King and raised an expectant brow.

"Ansin has Diviciacus' dagger, which means he has the ability to end my life when the time comes. I no longer need to appease the Seers. I assume you know how to use it properly?" he asked Ansin.

Ansin clicked his tongue and gave the old brow salute to King. "Yes. And I'll be naming the price."

"You threatened to kill me two moments ago. Now you wish to charge a price for it?" King snarled.

Ansin crossed his arms over his bare chest. "Yep."

King narrowed his pale gray eyes. "Better be reasonable. I could take your head and then your knife."

"Sorry to disappoint, but I'm just as hard to kill as you are. And the knife only works for the rightful owner."

These guys. These fucking guys. I shook my head. So King wanted to stick around long enough to raise Ariadna and derail her destiny. Then he wanted Ansin to end his life and be reunited with Mia and Arch.

Ansin wanted a family, but only as a backup in case Ariadna couldn't or wouldn't save his bloodline.

As for me, all I wanted was to make sure this little girl was born happy, healthy, safe and sound. I wanted her to have a choice and be free of the competing agendas around us. Because I was quickly learning that King and Ansin had both been right. Everyone wanted to own us, control us, and use us.

But would anyone ever just…love us? Maybe it was too late for me. But not for her. I had hope she could find another path even if she was born with an agenda of her own.

"This lovefest is super touching, guys, but I really hate this castle with a passion and don't want to spend another minute inside it. Can we just light it up and go?"

King nodded. "I'll find the car I drove here in and meet you outside. Do not be long, Seer."

"Jeni," I corrected with a sigh. What did these men have against using my name?

King walked past Ansin, being sure to give him a shoulder check on the way out.

Ansin raised two dark brows and scoffed.

These two were ticking time bombs. The moment they got what they wanted, one would try to kill the other.

I wasn't sure King would mind, but I would.

CHAPTER NINETEEN

"What are you thinking?" Ansin asked, still standing near the doorway of Sage's bedroom, shirtless, his meaty arms crossed over his scarred-up chest.

"About what?"

"I've never looked to my enemy to protect my interests. I've never looked to anyone. Now I have that baby and you to worry about."

"Am I really your interest, Ansin, or are you going to stab me in the back the moment you don't need me anymore?"

He flashed a wicked smile. His only smile. "Time will tell, my little treasure." He turned and left the room. "Like the bra, by the way. Very hot. I look forward to you saying yes for once when I ask you to remove it."

I couldn't help but smile. I knew he was talking about the dreams he'd had last night. An entire suck-fest of me telling him no. "Sorry. But I don't plan on ever saying yes!" I called out.

"We shall see." His voice faded with that last word.

He was so confident, wasn't he? Well, I wasn't. Nothing felt sure in this new situation.

In less than nine months, I would have a baby. Ansin was putting his hope in her to save a people who'd died two thousand years ago. King hoped she wouldn't save anyone except us. Here. Now.

One thing was for certain, the Seers were going to be pissed when the door to their reincarnation plan slammed shut in their faces. I had to prepare for the inevitable battle, and these two men were the only ones who could help.

But would they?

KING

Jeni was pregnant, and I would be a father again. To Ariadna. How was this possible? One thing was for certain, it explained what Jeni had been hiding and why her light seemed to flicker. The child was drawing from her energy. *Seers. They are a strange and unpredictable breed.*

Which was why I had very mixed feelings about Ariadna being reborn. Especially because they believed every wrong turn I had made was entirely my doing, when in reality, the long dark road I ultimately took in life had been because of them.

It had all started with Hagne over three thousand years ago. I had once been betrothed to her, but I didn't love her. She knew that. *They* knew that. I'd reluctantly agreed to the union for the sake of my people because the Seers had insisted. At the time, they protected our island from outside threats, so I did what good kings do: put the people first.

Then Mia arrived out of the blue, pregnant and holding a baby boy. She claimed to be my wife from the future, on the run from a group called Ten Club. I did not believe her initially, but eventually I succumbed to my feelings. Our connection was undeniable. Then Hagne, who'd always had a violent streak, tried to kill me in a fit of jealousy.

She missed.

Mia was gravely injured and bleeding out. To get the medical attention she needed, she would have to go home. The Seers offered to help my pregnant, dying, weak wife make the journey. For a sacrifice, of course. *Fucking Seers.* I would not be allowed to travel forward with Mia and Arch. Mia could never return to my time.

This meant if I ever wanted to see them again, I would have to stay alive for three thousand years. I would need to wait for Mia's life to start and for her to become a woman.

I should have let go. I should have died in my own time with the satisfaction of knowing I was loved by a good woman.

But I didn't.

I slid on a ring Mia had given me. With it, I would never age. I would live on. But not before the years of loneliness got to me. Everyone I ever knew or cared for was in the future or the past.

I went mad and killed every living Seer out of bitterness and hate. It had been their demand for a sacrifice that separated me from Mia.

But killing the Seers off hadn't been enough to satisfy my rage. I wanted them to suffer. Eventually, I created the beginnings of Ten Club—a group of ruthless individuals to assist me in my hunt for powerful objects. Over time the group evolved into something bigger, but I did find a way to resurrect those I held responsible for my suffering. I enslaved those Seers as a punishment, and Hagne had been at the top of my shit list.

It all ended badly, of course. But to say they played no part in it?

A fucking lie.

The Seers could have simply chosen to help Mia after she had been wounded. They could have helped me travel forward with my family. But no.

And for what?

So someday they could rise against me and attempt to take over Ten Club? So I could slaughter them all over again? So Hagne could escape me and kill Mia? So my children would die, too?

None of it made any sense. We'd all lost. We had all suffered immeasurably.

All I wanted now was to end the cycle of revenge, and to find peace, including for Ariadna, who had always been a concern to me. Seers who were denied the full life of a human before moving on grew tormented and bitter over time. Ariadna had never even made it out of the womb.

This rebirth—as impossible as it was—would be her chance, and I welcomed it. Even if I loathed the Seers, I still loved my children. I would do my best to free her fate from the grasp of those vengeful witches.

CHAPTER TWENTY

JENI

"How long are they planning to stay?" Dad asked as we cleaned up the kitchen after breakfast. I'd been back for three days—mostly sleeping, eating, and resting—but Dad just got home last night from hauling lumber a few states over, only to find two very dangerous men in his house who wouldn't stop arguing. Dad already knew about King, but Ansin was a new addition to a very uneasy situation.

"Fuck you, King. I'm not leaving her alone with you," Ansin yelled in the living room, which was just on the other side of the kitchen wall.

"You think you're any match for those Seers? Who the hell knows what they're planning," King responded.

"I can handle anything," Ansin threw back. "And if you don't believe me, allow me to demonstrate with my knife."

I sighed, and Dad gave me a worried look with his light brown eyes. "I'm glad they are both hell-bent on protecting you, because we both know I can't. But I worry about leaving you with them, Jeni."

Dad said he'd signed up for another haul tonight. It would only be a few days driving, but it meant I'd be alone with King and Ansin again.

I sighed. "I don't know what's going to happen, but they're the only chance I have. You staying around to watch over me isn't going to change anything. Plus, didn't you say you had plans with that…" I'd forgotten her name already. "The lady from the flower shop?"

"Yes, but I don't like this situation."

"I know, but what are you going to do? Fight the Seers yourself?"

"I don't actually understand how you became one. Your mother was, well, normal. I mean, she was wonderful, but no powers or anything like that. And from what I knew of your grandmothers, they weren't anything special, unless criticizing is a superpower."

"Funny." He'd loved his mother and mother-in-law, rest in peace. They'd spoiled him. As for their lack of gifts, it wasn't unusual for the Seer gene to skip multiple generations. "I'm sure if we searched hard enough, we'd discover some woman in our family was burned as a heretic or something." Hell, maybe even I was burned once. Now that we knew Seers could be reincarnated…

"You going to do something about them?" Dad jerked his head toward the living room as the argument between King and Ansin raged on. "This isn't healthy, Jeni. Maybe I need to take you out of here."

"There's nowhere to hide. Not from the Seers." I ran my fingers through my hair. "I'll take care of it."

I threw the dish towel over my shoulder and marched to the living room. "Guys, the fighting needs to stop. Okay? And I don't get what you're both so worried about. I highly doubt the Seers would go through all this trouble just to have me murdered here in my dad's living room while I'm still pregnant."

"I am not worried about them. Not yet," said King, eyeing Ansin.

I groaned with frustration. "If Ansin wanted me dead, he would have done it by now. He could have killed you, too, King."

The two men continued to stare each other down.

Nothing I said was going to change this, would it? This house wasn't big enough for two ancient alpha males who wanted to tear each other's throats out.

"Why don't you take turns?" I suggested. "Ansin can stay until my dad returns. Next week, King, you can stay when my dad goes away."

"And when your father is here?" King asked.

"You both go."

"He can't protect you," Ansin pointed out.

"No. But you guys make him feel uneasy, and I'm not about to subject him to that. He's been through enough."

"So what are we supposed to do, sleep on your front lawn?" King asked. "I'm not about to leave my daughter exposed."

"Figure it out," I said. "I'm going to shower now. I have to get ready."

"Where are you going?" King questioned.

"Doctor's appointment. And no. You can't come." I wasn't about to play happy domesticated coparents with him.

I headed toward the bathroom and immediately knew I was in hot water. King stood blocking the doorway. Ansin was beside him. Both towered over me with lean menacing muscles. One in a dress shirt, one in a T-shirt, neither of them fucking around.

If this were a rom-com movie, I'd be laughing. But this wasn't. King was deadly and evil as fuck. Ansin wasn't any better. Both only saw me for what I could give them, and it was starting to wear on my heart.

And this is just day three. But if I ran, if I tried to do this on my own, Ariadna might end up in the wrong hands. I couldn't have that.

My eyes shifted between the two tall men with dark hair, hypnotic eyes, and a masculine beauty only read about in fairy tales. One was refined, tailored and perfect, down to his eyelashes. The other was crude, rude, and scarred just about everywhere on his body. Both had powers. Both had agendas. Both were deadly and wanted me to obey.

Too bad for them. "Move," I said, losing my patience. "I need to shower."

"You're not leaving this house alone," said King.

"Then figure out which of you is going in the car, but neither is coming inside." I pushed past them, knowing they wouldn't actually hurt me. Not yet. But what would happen after Ariadna arrived?

I closed the bathroom door behind me.

"I heard that!" King barked. "It is an insult."

Is it, King? I snapped back. *Because I'm pretty sure you've told me, a few dozen times, that you'd kill me in a heartbeat if it served you.*

King didn't respond.

Yeah. Thought so. I undressed while King and Ansin started waving their red flags again, promising each other death and destruction.

I'd been stupid to think they could call a truce. This wasn't going to work. But if it came down to choosing sides, which one would it be?

Stop. Don't go there, I told myself as I ran the hot water. I would give anything right now for my mom to be here. I was pregnant and had no one to tell me what I should be feeling or if what I felt was normal. Doom. Fear. Happiness.

I shampooed my hair and rinsed. I conditioned and went to work on exfoliating with my shower glove, the coarseness triggering thoughts of my dream with Ansin.

His hands had been rough like this. So good. He knew exactly where to stroke, when to do it, and how hard. Not even I could duplicate his touch on my own, which made no sense. It had all been me in that dream, right? But the memories of his tongue, body, cock, everything, pushing in time to elevate my pleasure, had been better than any real experiences. At the very least, they rivaled my night with King.

"You look just as good as I imagined," said a deep voice.

"Ansin! What are you doing?" I pressed one arm across my breasts and held the other over my vagina.

"Just checking out my property," he said in a cold, serious voice.

"Can you please leave?"

"Thought you'd like to know King caved. I'll stay here. He'll fuck off."

What the hell? Sounded a little too easy. "What did you offer him?"

"That's between him and me."

I narrowed my eyes. "You agreed to kill him, didn't you?" Ansin said he'd name a price for releasing King from this world when the time came.

Ansin shrugged.

Sonofabitch. "Why did you do that?" As far as I was concerned, I'd need King as long as I lived. Not out of desperation, but because I'd spent the last few days thinking hard. "Ansin, if we successfully derail the Seers' plan for Ariadna, there's no reason to think they'll stop there. Not when they live forever in Seer-land. They'll try again to get their way. And they'll come after me."

He laughed dismissively. "You think I don't know that?"

"So you have a plan?"

"Yes, I'll stay here. When your dad is home, I'll sleep outside."

In other words, Ansin wasn't going to tell me. "Awesome. Bye-bye."

He closed the shower curtain, but I didn't hear the bathroom door open or shut.

"Ansin?"

The curtain pulled back again, only this time he stepped in.

Naked.

My breath stuck in my lungs. I'd never seen a man like him—huge, muscular, and so torn up. His pecs were two chiseled mounds, but his stomach was a washboard with scars. Every inch of his body looked like it had been forged in battle, steel shaped with battle-axes and war hammers.

"What are you doing?" I asked.

"Showering." He pushed past me, hogging the showerhead. I watched the water cascade down the ripples of his marred, deeply tanned back muscles. Again, I wanted to ask what had happened to him but was afraid to. Any answer he gave wouldn't be pretty.

Ansin turned his body and looked down at me, a lustful glimmer in his black and gold eyes.

The muscles between my legs tensed, recalling the release he'd given me in that dream. But this was real life.

And so is my body's reaction. Heat pooled in my core, and my skin erupted in goosebumps.

He stepped forward, his gaze locking on my mouth. I felt his desire to kiss me. I saw the image in his mind—him slamming me against the cool tile wall, fucking me hard. And me enjoying it.

My body trembled. My nipples pearled. I knew if I looked down at his cock, it would be hard and thick, and I might actually let him do what he was imagining.

No. I can't. "Enjoy the shower." I stepped out and grabbed my towel from the rack.

A deep chuckle sounded off from the other side of the curtain.

Asshole. He enjoyed getting a reaction out of me. Next time, I'd laugh at his dick. I'd laugh at him. Even if on the inside I was thinking about how badly I wanted what he had.

Bottom line, King already owned my heart. I wasn't going to allow Ansin to own the rest of me.

CHAPTER TWENTY-ONE

Ariadna was not much bigger than a jelly bean on the screen, but her heart sounded like a team of horses galloping wildly across an open plain. Strong. Unstoppable. I felt relieved knowing she was okay.

My health was good, too, despite the stress I'd been under. Unfortunately, unless I had a medical issue, I wasn't going to be making more trips to the doctor. The moment Dr. Nadine put the ultrasound wand inside, she started to sweat and get dizzy. I had to call for the nurse.

The baby was defending herself. I'd felt the heat in my womb and the air spike with electricity.

Was this normal? Did this happen when you carried a Seer?

I had no one to ask, and I didn't dare bring it up with King. That was the problem when you were surrounded by people you didn't trust.

I left the doctor's office, and Ansin drove me home in the very large, very decked-out armored Hummer he'd obtained. I didn't bother asking where he got it.

"Are you certain you don't want to stay in your new house?" he asked as we headed back.

"Sorry?"

"I told you I would ensure you wanted for nothing, little treasure." His intense eyes remained fixed on the road and mirrors, constantly searching for threats.

"You stole a house?" He had no shame.

"I bought it. Legally."

"That's surprising. I thought you didn't believe in owning things." Except me, apparently.

"A peace offering. I know you don't approve of my philosophy regarding material possessions," he replied.

"Nope. Sure don't." And I wasn't about to get all gooey and squishy over this guy just because he'd purchased a house. I knew what he was. A mistake.

Now that I'd seen the baby, reality had come crashing down on me. Hard. What kind of world would I be bringing her into? Ansin and King as our protectors? No, this wouldn't do.

"Are you ever going to trust me?" he asked.

"No."

"Good." He smiled, weaving in and out of traffic, driving like he meant business. "You shouldn't trust anyone."

"You sound just like King," I muttered.

"I may want to kill the man, but he's no fool."

"You sure about that?" I threw back.

"What exactly is the story between you guys,

anyway?"

I shrugged. "Why do you care?"

"I'm going to end his life. Maybe not today, but someday. Even he won't argue with that. I suppose I'd like to understand the dynamics of your relationship—what it will mean to you when I end him."

"How thoughtful," I said sarcastically. "The answer is: I don't know. I met him. I felt a connection. Then I discovered his soul is anchored to me, and since us Seers can't ever really die, he won't die until that bond is broken somehow."

"Which means he can't be with his wife and son."

"Yes," I replied.

"So you love him, he loves her, and you're standing in his way."

"Not me. The ancient Seers," I pointed out.

"And what happens when I finally end his life and break that bond? How will you feel?"

"I don't know," I lied. I knew exactly how I'd feel. Devastated.

"Do you think you'll still love him, or are your feelings a product of the bond?" he asked.

I'd contemplated that question a thousand times but came to the conclusion my love had nothing to do with our supernatural bond. I guessed because it wasn't love at first sight with King. If anything, I'd wanted to run away and never look back when we first met. "What's it to you?"

"You are going to be my wife and the mother of

my children. I'd like to know where your loyalties lie."

"They lie with my baby."

"Will you always choose your children over everyone else?"

"Why wouldn't I?" Not as if I'd place Ansin over them. He frightened me. He was brutal and coldhearted. As for my other feelings for him, those were sexual. They weren't the sorts of emotions I could base trust on.

Ansin's eyes grew intense as he barreled onto the freeway. "Funny, you and I have the same weakness: family."

"Family's a weakness? I don't see it that way." My family gave me strength.

"You will. Especially when those Seers come calling with their list of demands."

"They're not my family." How could they be when I would never trust them?

"They're your blood. And you, my little treasure, won't have an easy decision to make when they ask you to give up every piece of yourself for what they want. You'll feel the pull."

"Are you speaking from experience?"

"Yes."

"What choice did you make?" I asked.

"I'll let you know when I make it."

That was the moment I understood there was more to Ansin's story—things he hadn't told me about resurrecting his bloodline.

"If Ariadna grows up and agrees to help you save your people, what will change for you? What will you lose?" I asked.

He said nothing.

"Well, if it means anything coming from me, I hope it all works out for you."

"It won't."

"How do you know that?" I asked.

"Because the Seers are right. Everything comes with a price, Jeni. Everything. Mine will be great."

Did he believe this path would lead to his death? Sure the hell sounded like it.

I contemplated using my gift to see his future but quickly changed my mind. Did I really want to watch him die? No. I didn't. And clearly, he knew the price of his decision. If it was his fate, there wasn't much I could do.

I looked out the car window, thinking about that story Circe told of the girl in the ravine. If all I wanted was for this baby to be free, what would be the price? Or was her fate sealed, and I simply had to accept it?

CHAPTER TWENTY-TWO
ANSIN

Over eight long months, Jeni still hadn't agreed to live with me in the house I purchased, but ironically, I discovered I required distance anyway. I'd had to move into an RV outside in the driveway.

It was impossible to keep a clear head around her after the baby began to grow. The Seer she carried was unlike anything I'd ever come across. Powerful was an understatement. My people, the Seers, and King paled in comparison to the energy it gave off.

I knew King had been sensing the same, keeping his distance, and not because we'd made a deal—he'd back off and let me be Jeni's guardian in exchange for his execution. *"When I am not needed by this baby, it will be my time to go,"* he said. A win-win for all, in my mind. Of course, King remained in town since Jeni carried his daughter incarnate.

As long as I didn't see the fucker.

This world wasn't big enough for the two of us. Not in the long run. Hell, maybe it was only big enough for that child and Jeni, whom I'd been observing from a distance. My little treasure was determined, each day practicing her skills. I knew she was preparing to fight. The question was, who?

When King was around, I watched her fight her feelings for him. She believed it was love, but I knew better. The Seers had a hand in it, and the sooner Jeni was free of King, the sooner she'd be free to become what she was born to be. Mine.

But truthfully, I didn't want to own her. I didn't want to manipulate her. I'd grown to respect her in ways I never imagined. Jeni was a fighter, and I sensed she'd be a force to be reckoned with after the baby came. I'd grown excited by what we could be together.

I'd even begun to wonder if saving my people was the correct choice. Someday, if Ariadna went back and stopped their slaughter, it meant I would never have been cursed by Mother. I would die thousands of years ago as nature intended.

Now, for the first time, I was thinking about what I wanted, and the price to have it.

"Ansin! Ansin!" Jeni called out from her bedroom. I was in the backyard, doing one of the many lowly chores her father demanded of me since he was rarely home.

I rushed inside and found her sitting on the edge of her bed.

"What is it?" I panted my words, reaching for my knife.

"I heard screaming." King appeared behind me.

"What are you doing here?" I seethed.

"I happened to be in the neighborhood," King said.

"Stop. Please. I need to get to the hospital. My water broke." Jeni pressed on her stomach. "It hurts. Something's wrong."

The baby wasn't due for another few weeks. "I'll drive."

"Like hell." King scooped up Jeni and marched toward the front door.

Fucking King. I couldn't wait for the day I'd get to remove his head.

I rushed outside and opened the back passenger door of King's fucking ridiculous luxury sedan. I hated everything about him—his obsession with material things and wealth. I was equally as wealthy, but all I owned was a house. Yes, it was a twelve-million-dollar house on the beach near Miami, but I'd bought it for Jeni.

She still hadn't seen it. She said she wasn't ready to think that far ahead.

I got in the back seat with Jeni, more excited than I should be. Here I was, over two thousand years old. I'd seen people come and go—some by my own hand. To me, life was transitory and meaningless except for the lives of my people. But here I was, looking forward to a Seer being born. She wasn't even mine.

King started the engine.

"Drive carefully," I said, taking Jeni's hand. "And get that fucking thing out of here."

A dark shadow hovered around the car. By now I'd figured out what it was.

"I didn't invite him," King said.

What the hell did that mean? Was King's soul here to watch the birth of this Seer?

Fuck, this is too crazy. Even for me.

KING

Mia, if you can somehow hear me, I want you to know I will stay until she is ready to fend for herself. After that, I'm leaving. I miss you far too much.

Mia was beyond my reach now, but a part of me hoped she felt what was about to happen. The daughter who'd had her life stolen by a Seer in an act of revenge against me would have another chance, and I couldn't help but feel anxious to witness it before I left this world.

I glanced in the rearview mirror. Jeni's face was pale.

"King! Oh God. It hurts." Jeni curled into a tight ball in the back seat with Ansin, cradling her stomach.

"We are almost there. Try to use your gifts, Seer. Relax," I said.

"Something's...wrong..." Jeni moaned.

"Is she bleeding? Is she hemorrhaging?" I asked

Ansin.

"How would I know? I don't see anything. *Ariadna, you are to keep breathing. Do you hear me? You are to fight,*" Ansin said.

"Do not use that mindfuck crap on my daughter," I snarled. Ansin's tribe had been filled with archaic pagan witches. Primitive. Savage. I knew because I had come across them a few thousand years ago. Likely before Ansin was born.

"Do you have any better ideas, King? If yes, I'm all ears," Ansin said.

"Oh God. Hurry. Hurry," Jeni whimpered.

"We're here." I slammed on the brakes, and Ansin jumped from the car and disappeared inside. He reemerged with several men and a gurney. They removed Jeni from the vehicle and took her inside.

As I sat behind the steering wheel, a wave of darkness washed over me. Was it my imagination? Because I swore I felt my soul pushing against my skin, as if trying to get in.

The air does not feel right. An energy buzzed all around us, almost like a warning. Something bad was about to happen. I felt it in my bones.

CHAPTER TWENTY-THREE
JENI

My pulse raced, my body screamed with pain, and my mind couldn't find shelter from any of it. The only way out was through. I had to push.

The nurse got an IV into my arm and an oxygen mask strapped to my face. The small room was filled with people who, for lack of a better term, looked uneasy.

Yes. Medical professionals in an ER. Looking uneasy.

Something was wrong with the baby.

Ariadna. Please. Just let them do their job, sweetie. They're going to help you come out safely.

A doctor entered the room and quickly introduced himself, explaining the situation. The baby's heart rate was erratic. They didn't know why.

"Jeni, you're already fully dilated, so you have to push," he said.

I was? But how? I'd only started having pain about twenty minutes ago.

He added, "We'll give you a few minutes, but if

the baby doesn't come out quickly, we'll have to do a C-section."

I didn't want to be cut open like I'd seen Sage do to King in my nightmares over the last eight months. "If anyone gets near me with a scalpel, I'll kill them," I growled. "I'll get her out. On my own."

The contractions hit again, and I pushed into the pain. "Ahhh!" I shrieked in agony, feeling like my pelvis was cracking, like my insides were shredding and my outsides were tearing.

Ansin stormed into the small room, holding his knife. "What's going on…"

"Put that away," I barked.

Thankfully the staff didn't notice.

Ansin came over and took my hand, lowering his voice and speaking in a calm tone. *"You don't feel a thing. You're safe. You're going to push her out now."*

His words sank into my skull, and my body went numb. He'd just used that mindfuck trick. "Why? Why use that on me now?"

"Because you needed it."

The next wave hit, but this time, it didn't hurt. I pushed, knowing this was happening all too fast. No one delivered a baby in five minutes. Not their first time. It was like she wanted to get out and wasn't about to wait for anyone. Why was I surprised? *King's kid.*

"Here comes the head," the doctor said just as King appeared in the back of the room, his pale gray eyes watching with intensity.

"One more. Give us one more," the doctor said and pulled the baby out. The doctor clipped and cut the umbilical cord, and the nurse immediately took her to clean her face and nose over on a little table.

I didn't know how I felt about King and Ansin seeing something so…intimate, but all that mattered was Ariadna.

"Is she okay?" I panted.

"He is just fine," said the nurse.

"Congratulations. It's a beautiful baby boy," the doctor said.

My heart skipped a beat. "A boy?" There must've been a mistake.

"Well done, Jeni. Well done." Ariadna appeared at my side, looking as real and alive as ever with flowing blonde locks and those hypnotic brown eyes I remembered from my vision. I was still in the bed, but now the room was empty. Of people and equipment.

It's the white room. I'd seen it in my visions.

"Where did everyone go? And what's happening?" I pointed to the baby. "That's supposed to be you."

Ariadna shook her head slowly. "I'm sorry but no."

"I don't…" My words faded off. Was I tripping? Had Ansin done something to me?

Ariadna flashed a venomous smile. "You've given us what we need to start over, what was meant to be from the beginning: a baby boy with King's blood and yours, Hagne."

"Hagne?" I frowned.

"You thought I would be the first Seer brought back, but it was you, Hagne. Your penance for killing my mother, me, and my baby brother that night of the Seer massacre."

My head started to pound. "I'm not Hagne. I'm Jeni. And I would never hurt a child." There had to be some mistake.

"I assure you, you would. And for your crime of killing a Seer, the highest crime a Seer can commit, you will live out the remainder of your life paying penance. You will love a king who will never love you back. You will raise his child, who will serve as a constant reminder of what you've done wrong. And you will belong to another man who will make you suffer in ways you cannot imagine because you are incapable of loving him back."

My eyes filled with tears. "I didn't do anything. I don't know what you're talking about. I'm not Hagne. And I saw you being born in my vision. What's happening?"

"Don't worry, Hagne, I'll be along soon. Just not today. In the meantime, take care of our lord. He is meant to do great things for us."

What the fuck? What's happening?

"Jeni?" King's voice rang in my ears. I was back in the ER.

I looked up at King's shocked face and then down at the baby in my arms with a wash of thick black hair and blue eyes. He was the spitting image of King. "He-he was what they were after all along." I shook my head. "But... I'm not Hagne. Ariadna said I'm Hagne. What's happening, King?"

He looked down at the boy in my arms. "They fooled you. They fooled me. And they got what they wanted."

"But I'm not her, King. I would never...kill...I would never..." The pieces began sliding into place—why I loved him without reason. Our connection. The pain I suffered for my heart.

I might not remember being Hagne or what she'd done, but I felt the pain they wanted me to suffer. I understood Ariadna's disdain for me.

"I'm sorry, King. I'm so sorry. I don't know what's happening, but—"

"No one sees anything." Ansin swooped behind King and sliced his throat. Blood poured from the open wound, and King dropped to the floor.

I opened my mouth to yell, but no sound came out. The nurse and doctor stood still, staring at the wall like zombies.

All I could hear was the gentle purr of the baby boy in my arms and the sound of King gurgling his final breaths.

"Why? Why, Ansin?" I whispered, unable to comprehend what just happened. My arms and hands trembled with anger. I felt my heart shattering deep inside my chest.

"I saw it in his eyes. I felt his rage in the air.

Whoever this Hagne is or was, whoever you are, he was about to end your life, Jeni."

"You can't know that. His soul is anchored to mine and—"

"And he didn't give a shit. He was about to send you on your way. I've seen the faces of men when their rage overtakes them. It was him or you." Ansin shrugged. "I chose."

He snapped his fingers at the nurse and doctor, who woke. "See that Jeni and her baby boy are taken care of. Dispose of that body in an incinerator. Immediately." Ansin flashed a remorseful look my way. "I'm sorry it worked out like this. I'll see you in a few months to plan our next steps."

"Steps?" I spoke, but I wasn't really all there. How could I be? The man I loved was dead on the floor. But my love was a curse, a burden for crimes I didn't recall.

"Oh," Ansin added, "and congratulations. He is a beautiful boy. Will make a good addition to my arsenal someday. Or a lord of Seers. We'll see who wins."

What did he mean by that?

The infant in my arms began to cry, and I screamed at the top of my lungs at the body on the floor, "King! Wake up! You can't go!"

But he could and he had. King was dead.

TO BE CONTINUED

Don't miss the final piece of the King series.

For more: www.mimijean.net/neverkings

AUTHOR'S NOTE

Hello, King fans!

All right, raise your hand if you saw that twist coming? It's a boy! And whoa! Seems like he's going to be a powerful guy.

But now the question remains, is King really dead?

If yes, does he get to see Mia and Arch?

Are the Seers good or bad?

And what the heck do the Seers plan to do with Lord King?

OMG! So many questions!

I will confess that I did write a few more chapters, which answer at least one of those questions, but then I decided to pause here. Mostly because I want to give a lot of pages to a certain event we've all been waiting for. Say no more. Say no more!

As for more King books, I have nothing planned after *NEVER KING'S* (Coming 2022). Of course, many of you know I never planned to go beyond the trilogy. Then came *Mack* and *Ten Club*. But once I decided King's lies to Mia couldn't go unpunished, it kicked off three new books (a very, verrrrry extended epilogue.): *Dead King, Lord King, Never King's.*

So yeah, *Never King's* will be the end of the "epilogue."

Can I promise I won't write more King in ten years? No, but this three-book leg of the storyline has a firm, definitive ending. No cliff. I knew exactly how it would end when I began, and I think you're going to flip. Juicy!

Another fun note about the book covers, for those of you who are into symbolism. Notice that the first three books in the series are dark and gloomy, each cover with a different color palette. Red, purple, blue. In these final three books, the background is white because the stories are about King's journey to redemption. Also notice the color of the smoke in each cover. Red, purple, blue—just like the first books in the trilogy. (The *Never King's* cover, at least a partial, can be seen here: www.mimijean.net/ neverkings.html) Obviously red is anger, purple is enlightenment, and blue is royal. Because, yeah, he's a king. Our man deserves some blue after what I've put him through. Hahaha!

EITHER WAY! Keep an eye out for more King in

2022, along with more Huff (our superhero) and Emily (from M.O. Mack) along with two new series! *Wall Men* will be a horror romance. I've always wanted to try my hand at scaring the hell out of readers. Because, fun! Muahaha! Our insane immortals, including Cimil, will also be back in *The Immortal Tailor*. I can't wait. (Write faster, Mimi! Faster!)

Be sure you're signed up for alerts of upcoming releases so you don't miss out:
www.mimijean.net/get-news-from-mimi

And now onto your favorite part. FREE BOOK-MARKS!

STEP ONE: Email me at Mimi@mimijean.net

STEP TWO: Provide your complete shipping info (include the country if you're outside the US).

STEP THREE: If you wrote a review for *Lord King,* because you loved it and are one of those cool people who show support for your favorite authors, be sure to provide a link or screenshot. I will do my very best to include extra goodies. I run out of magnets fast! It's first ask, first get! But you will get a big THANK YOU from me either way.

STEP FOUR: Give me about 3–4 weeks. I'm pretty slow at getting snail mail out, but I do get to it. I send email confirmations once they go.

Thank you to all the fans who've stuck with King over all these years! He's been an amazing character to write. I never know where his messed-up life will take me!

HUGS,
Mimi

PS – Want to hear the *Lord King* playlist? **Go to my Spotify list.** Or search for my username "mimi-jeanpamfiloff" to see the playlists for all my books!

ACKNOWLEDGMENTS

Thank you, team Mimi! Book #54! Woohoo. As always, I appreciate every ounce of help I get in bringing these books to life. Stephanie, LD, Paul, Pauline, Su, Kylie, Jaycee, and Joan.

Thank you to my family for always finding little and big ways to show your love.

With Love,
Mimi

ABOUT THE AUTHOR

MIMI JEAN PAMFILOFF is a *New York Times* bestselling author who's sold over one million books around the world. Although she obtained her MBA and worked for more than fifteen years in the corporate world, she believes that it's never too late to come out of the romance closet and follow your dreams.

Mimi lives with her Latin lover hubby, two pirates-in-training (their boys), and their three spunky dragons (really, just very tiny dogs with big attitudes) Snowy, Mini, and Mack, in the vampire-unfriendly state of Arizona.

She hopes to make you laugh when you need it most and continues to pray daily that leather pants will make a big comeback for men.

Sign up for Mimi's mailing list for giveaways and new release news!

www.ingramcontent.com/pod-product-compliance
Lightning Source LLC
Chambersburg PA
CBHW061246120726
48001CB00001B/173